TUTTLEBO[

G. Derek Jones.

Published by
"Heart of Oak" The Manse,
St Peter, Jersey.
JE3 7AA

Tel: - 44 (0) 1534 481479
Email: - heartofoak@safe-mail.net

ISBN> 0-9549462-4-3

First Edition published in Great Britain 2006.

Copyright Mr G D Jones.

The Author asserts the moral right to be identified as the author of this book. No part of this book may be reproduced without the author's written permission.

A Catalogue edition of this book is available from the British Library.

Printed and bound for Heart of Oak by: - Lightning source UK LTD.

6 Precedent Drive, Rooksley, Milton Keynes, Bedfordshire. MK13 8PR, UK

Cover Photo from Freefoto.com a Shropshire village.

To contact the author directly Tel: - 01948 860237

Or write to: -

Mr. G D Jones, The Deran, Cuddington Heath, Malpas, Cheshire. SY14 7EN.

TUTTLEBOROUGH TALES

Chapter: -

1.	Tuttleborough	4
2.	Tuttleborough Children	10
3.	Winter Tale	12
4.	Sol Hatton	15
5.	Nathan's Pig	19
6.	Eli Welch	26
7.	The Widow Ellie	30
8.	Norm Knew His Onions	34
9.	Gertrude Twigg	37
10.	Billy Bufton	44
11.	The Village Concert	51
12.	A Royal Fête	61
13.	The Feud	71
14.	One Arm Jack	75
15.	A Case of Black & White	81
16.	Aunt Alice	86
17.	Wilf's Gift	93
18.	George	104
19.	Dewdrop Tonks	110
20.	Tuttleborough F.C.	114

Tuttleborough

Tuttleborough was a recondite little village tucked away in a fold of gentle hills which rolled in languid beauty towards the Welsh border.

A stolid Norman church looked down with patriarchal concern over a cluster of cottages and scattered small holdings. A little way from its centre, on a slightly higher elevation stood 'The Manor' which had been the home for five generations of Pitchfords. The present incumbent, Major Erasmus Pitchford had inherited all but one of the local small holdings, nearly half of the cottages and most of the arable and grazing land. Lady Day was his big pay day.

In the early 1830's a kindly benefactor had donated one hundred pounds to convert a stone barn into a village school. The rigid system of regimented lessons at the school supplemented the joyful natural education every child enjoyed as they played their way through fields, lanes and woodlands. The names of every tree, flower and animal became familiar, and remembered each returning season more readily than the repetitious chanting of multiplication tables every school morning.

Mr Leese the ageing headmaster would conduct the melancholy choir as though he were Father Superior at a monastery.

When Mrs Lovatt took over the general store in 1926, the inventory of stock included a score of left handed potato peelers, eight rolls of wire netting, fence posts, gin traps, billy cans, flat irons and twenty one pairs of hobnailed boots ranging in size from six to thirteen. An enquiry for anything she did not have in stock always promoted the same answer. "Come back next week". Mrs Lovatt never let a prospective customer down.

Some cottages had their own supply of well-water linked to taps in the kitchen. Most however carried fresh supplies by the bucket full each day from the village pump. Villagers casually meeting at the pump provided a vital means of communication. Births, marriages and deaths were the most popular and fertile topics of conversation.

Born and raised Tuttleborough residents were justly proud of their village. Parochial in outlook they resented change. The simple philosophy that 'if it was good enough for Gran it's good enough for me' had slowed down the introduction of labour saving devices both in the home and on the farm. They had an instinctive suspicion of any thing modern. When the wireless first arrived it was blamed for a drop in milk production. A slight increase in the birth rate coincided with the arrival of the first motor powered vehicles: they were not blamed directly but the old women expressed their doubts.

It was not only machines that were looked upon with suspicion. Wellington boots had been available since the early twenties, but few land workers were willing to swap the well greased hobnailed boots for such unproven footwear. Bud Edge claimed Wellingtons would never catch on "cos they clemed the legs". One had to spend a day in the corn harvest wearing such revolutionary footwear to understand what he meant.

It is not unreasonable to presume that the advent of war in 1939 had a softening effect on the farmer's indifference to mechanisation.

A national pride in doing their bit for the war effort reluctantly overcame the love for their faithful heavy horses. A paranoid schizophrenic little dictator had done what no British politician could have achieved with legislation.

The economy of the village revolved around agriculture and contributory industries. Life for the older working generation was simple in plan but hard in physical labour. After spending a day out in the field, back bent, muscles strained, a labourer would return home heavy booted, refresh himself with a splash of water and a slurp of tea before spending an hour tending his own cottage crops. The flowering plants were left to the woman's tender care.

The simple rule which governed the life of the agricultural worker was
'if it was daylight you worked, if it was dark you rested'.

The men were the breadwinners, the women stayed at home to provide every need for husband and family. Unquestioned confidence in the system created a strong family unit.

The village had many craftsmen, each a master of his trade. Most had followed in their father's footsteps, learning from the cradle. All the village girls could cook, sew, darn and knit well before school leaving age at fourteen.

It was rare to find an adult who had a hobby unless a few extra coppers could be made from it.

Tom Wells carved the most intricate designs on walking sticks during winter evenings by the light of oil lamps. Bob Tutt painted pictures of wild flowers and birds on every empty tin he could lay his hand on. He got the idea after spending an afternoon on a canal barge. He had fallen into the canal when fishing, been dragged our by a bargee and invited to dry out by the pot stove. The gaily painted utensils of the canal dwellers had inspired him. Both Tom and Bob made the occasional sale which gave almost a hundred percent profit.

Si Oakley however regularly sacrificed himself in order to feed his loft of pigeons. He kept a meagre flight of about twenty birds, mostly red chequered. "That colour has the most stamina" Si would explain to any probing questioner. In spring he would regularly cycle twenty miles from the village, a basket of young birds strapped to the carrier. Once released the birds circled and made for home. By the time Si got back the birds were ready for their next training stint. When asked if his birds ever won any races he would reply "them that can't fly make a good pie".

Almost every cottage had the luxury of a wireless set by the mid nineteen thirties. Only the Midge sisters refused to consider ever having such an instrument of the devil's making in their house. It was the villager's one way link to the outside world.

Radios, as they later came to be called took over from the daily newspaper, but did not affect its sales. Radios were not designed to hang on the back of the privy door, to be wedged between the vest and shirt on frosty mornings; to lay under carpets, or to wrap the autumn apple crop before storage.

The only recreational activities for the adults were those which they devised for themselves. Occasionally a dance would be held in the church hall but only since the liberal thinking Rev. Sequera had replaced the hard line tombstone faced Rev. Collie.

Christmas, a wedding, more frequently a christening, the harvest supper and the annual summer fête were the only other occasions people had to celebrate.

Tuttleborough children had the same hopes and aspirations as other village youngsters who lived in the border counties, though limited when compared to their counterparts in the towns.

The Tuttleborough Children.

Children's games were mainly traditional and seasonal. Whipping tops, marbles and hop scotch each had a short season of interest interspersed with intricate combinations of skipping games by the girls and cigarette card flicking by the boys.

When the horse chestnut trees shed their shiny brown cobs, the broken remains of conker contests littered the school playground.

Most boys carried a catapult, its fangs cut from a sapling ash. Many crafted long bows from a holly staff or wild rose brier. The arrows were made from straight nut sticks cut from the hazel coppice. Apart from a short length behind the sharpened point the bark was stripped away by pen knife before inserting and securing a goose feather Fight in a slit at the opposite end.

Occasionally the catapult did claim a few victims for the cooking pot. The bow however was more frequently used to send a silver cloud of thistle down blowing across the fields after a direct hit.

The Tuttleborough school boys had devised their own unique version of Fox and Hounds, a favourite game of long standing with country lads. In autumn, when day-light was all but gone they would meet under the big oak near the blacksmith's forge. On the spin of a coin two contestants were nominated as foxes while the rest, usually five or six in number became the hounds. The rules were simple. Boundaries were set which encompassed approximately a square mile. The two foxes were given ten minutes to disappear into the blackness of the night. If they had not been tracked down by the hounds within an hour, the foxes were deemed to have won. If however they were caught, the penalty was a ducking under the village pump.

On one of these night time chases young Tim Griffies and Charlie Thomas realised that the hounds had got their scent and were closing in. They took to their heels across an open field. Simultaneously at full speed they met an immovable object. Legs and arms flying they sailed over its top to pick themselves up at the exact moment the object arose to loom above them uttering a disgruntled long low moo - oo - oo.

Under normal circumstances country lads have no fear of cattle. To run into a cow in the middle of a field on a night as black as a bag was an experience they carefully avoided in the future.

WINTER TALE

An inch of snow is worth a cart load of muck so the old country saying goes. Its wisdom can be seen in the yield of the following season's crops.

To the children a few inches of snow and a sharp frost was worth hours of pleasure careering down the hillside on homemade sledges. Singles, doubles, everyone piled on at the same time, sitting down, lying down, facing backwards, standing on one leg; every variation and permutation that it was possible to devise for travelling by sledge from the top to the bottom was experimented with.

A village philosopher once said 'a country lad can hear grass grow and smell a trout in a stream but the last thing he sees is danger'.

With the snow in prime condition and the run extending after each succeeding ride, eight lads bound tight together on the biggest sledge were going for the village record. Under their combined weight the sledge gathered momentum and began to accelerate at an unbelievable speed. As the boundary fence loomed ominously, sledge riders were shot off into the snow like peas from a pod, until only poor Phil Hopper remained. Ashen faced and wide eyed he stoically held on. The sledge disappeared under the fence wires, slid down the cop and crashed onto the road.

The brave driver was left untidily wrapped round a post, the white snow slowly turning crimson. The record had been broken. For the next week young Phil, the champion, walked round the village proudly displaying his bandaged head.

February of 1939 heralded a winter equal in its relentless cruel severity to that of 1918 so the old men said. Exploded eggs frozen in the nest boxes were collected each morning from the hen coups. Hungry foxes hunted the domestic cats. Icicles hung like giant tubular bells from every guttering. Trees groaned under the weight of frozen snow. Some split their bark like the waistcoat of a squire after Christmas dinner. The brook gave up the struggle and lay like a sleeping silver snake across the countryside. Only the water in the wells resisted the onslaught. Every dew pond and pit froze solid. Even Old Hanna's Pool, a ten acre expanse of sporting pike water froze for only the second time in living memory, deep enough for bonfires to have little effect upon it.

News of such an unusual event spread to the surrounding villages and the nearby town. Saturday afternoons transformed

Old Hanna's Pool to a scene like a Peter Breughel painting brought magically to life.

One weekend when a group of young gentlemen from a public school arrived bristling with shiny ice skates, hockey sticks and a genuine puck, was long remembered by the local lads.

Having tired of watching the extravagant exhibitionist skills of the visitors, the local lads challenged them to a game. With loud guffaws and comments on how they would give the bumpkins a lesson they would not forget, the challenge was accepted.

Within minutes it was evident that the right equipment and breeding was no match for hobnailed boots, sticks cut from the woodland, a joyful ignorance of the rules and a score to settle. The bumpkins were jubilant over their victory but could not understand why the bruised, battered and bleeding opponents should have shook hands with them all before limping back home.

Mr Lees the school master later explained it to them. So it could be said that both teams learned a valuable lesson for life that day. Winter relented during the early days of April, giving Dewie Jenkins permanent dew drop a chance to thaw.

SOL HATTON

Sol Hatton had been a wheelwright all his working life. At the demise of his craft he took to general carpentry, mending anything from a barn door to a broken wooden doll.

Despite being a brilliant craftsman and one of the most honest, genuine, cheerful, outward going characters in the village Sol did not readily find casual work.

Some said he was accident prone, others that he was a jinx, because he had been born on Friday 13th April. A rumour was whispered that his mother had been given the eye by a gypsy woman when she was eight months heavy with Sol, which accounted for his misfortunes.

It was not that Sol suffered personal injury. The unnerving fact was that strange things just happened when he was in the vicinity. As a school boy, the blackboard and easel would collapse if he was asked to clean it. An aimless kick of the ball in the playground would send his boot crashing through a window or smashing into someone's head.

As years went by the trail of havoc grew. A goal post collapsed when Sol leaned against it during an important inter-village match.

Jerry Bell the game keeper was sent plunging into Old Hanna's Pool while Sol was helping him to land a massive pike.

Part of a wall collapsed at Rose Cottage while he was fitting a new door frame. When collecting a new iron shod barrow from the shop he ran over Mrs Wilson's foot and broke her big toe.

The traction engine and thrashing box arrived at the Manor House Home Farm for the last time in late March 1938. Only able to raise a team of six fit men, the farm bailiff reluctantly asked Sol to make the number up to the required seven. With the regulars all at their preferred stations Sol was asked to take the thatch pins out of the stack. He had only withdrawn a dozen or so when the ladder slipped. Down came Sol like a November apple to land square on Ben Able's shoulders. Ben was helped away with a suspected broken collar bone. Sol picked himself up, muttered 'that was lucky' and set off up the ladder again.

With one man short, the bailiff enlisted the help of two of the older school lads from the bunch who had gathered for the annual sport of rat donging when the stack dwindled to the last few layers of sheaves.

The lads were asked to take the hundred weight grain sacks from the chute and stack them in the granary. Sol was relegated to the worst job of all, chaff clearing.

Once the engine had got enough steam up and the pressure was right, the pitches and feeders set to with a will. No one could shout above the thunderous noise of the steam engine and thrashing box. Any communication was performed by hand signal.

Ten minutes or so into the operation, the lacing on the drive belt broke. Within minutes of it being repaired Bryn Trevor, standing in the drum dropped his cap, to see it emerge in a thousand shreds mingled with the chaff.

As one man the workers began signalling to the bailiff and pointing towards Sol, who unconcerned, kept shovelling away at the heap of chaff.

The bailiff walked towards Sol and cupping his hands to his mouth said something in Sol's ear. A few minutes later he was walking towards the village carrying an empty oil can.

Upon his return, the same procedure sent him in the direction of the Manor kitchen, soon to return with Billy cans of tea.

With various clever ploys the bailiff kept Sol busy running errands until late afternoon by which time a ton and a half of grain had been safely stored and the excited yelps of terriers and dull thud of heavy knobbed sticks added their distinctive sounds to end the occasion.

Nathan's Pig

One of the very few men in the village who did not sport a sobriquet was Nathan Pegg. This was surprising because Nathan was the local vermin exterminator. Given such an opportunity one would have expected the fertile minds of the young school boys to have christened him Ratty or Mole or even Smelly.

It was claimed that he could smell a rat at thirty paces. It was a definite fact that Nathan's presence could be detected at more than thirty paces if the wind was in the right direction.

Nathan Pegg resembled a mobile midden heap. Tufts of wiry grey hair stuck like old thatch through a hole in his shiny cap, the original pattern of which had long been obscured by a thick layer of grime. A tightly knotted red neckerchief clashed with his ruddy to purple complexion. The stubble around his jowls resembled a badly harvested cornfield. A thicket of tawny crisp hair burst through the front of an off grey calico button less shirt. It had long since lost the battle to encompass his powerful barrel chest. A fusty jacket hung from his shoulders, pulled shapeless by the weight of a rural museum contained in its pockets.
Plus fours were loosely held in place by a broad leather belt, the buckle from which could have doubled as a trivet. The trousers were not washed until they began to crack. First World War

putties bound his lower legs then disappeared into a pair of size twelve hob nailed boots.

Being a bachelor (some said not by choice) he lived alone at Latch Cottage, an unkempt hovel on the confines of the village.

A one-eyed ginger tom cat had taken up lodgings there, mainly because its adversity did not affect its ability to catch as many mice as it needed without setting paws outside the door.

The sleek brindle whippet which followed his master wherever he went was obviously immune to his environment.

As was the custom with cottagers Nathan kept a pig in a sty, just a few yards from the back door. When the pig reached ten score in weight it was slaughtered and became an essential part of the household budget.

When the time arrived another piglet had taken its place. Nathan would cajole a farmer who was visiting the beast market to bring him back a 'rit'. These could frequently be obtained for as little as a shilling or on some occasions sixpence if they had only an even chance of survival.

Late one spring; unable to find anyone going to the auction Nathan mounted his errand-boy type carrier bicycle and set off to do his own purchasing.

During the early evening of that same day he returned, pushing his bike through the village with a tired whippet in his wake and a smug faced piglet sitting contentedly in the carrier.

Whether it was the fact that he had been given the pig, or the well mannered way it had behaved on the journey home, is not certain; but from the following day onward Nathan set out on his grizzly business each morning with the pig as an extra companion.

By the late afternoon he would return, the bike transformed into a travelling gibbet. The carcass of moles, rabbits and the occasional hares; hanging in pairs from the carrier giving the impression of a pig wearing a macabre skirt. The dimensions of the carrier remained constant; the dimensions of the pig did not.

As spring slipped into summer, in turn over taken by autumn, the sight of a nearly fully grown pig with the assured air of an Orwellian survivor had been accepted by the villagers.

Nathan's eccentricity unwittingly carved a niche in the village folklore. To this day anyone who makes a bad purchase is said to have "bought a pig on a bike". An unlikely happening is qualified by "and pigs might cycle".

From the cot, infants are told the story of the "two little pigs" and the one that got away on a bike.

There was just one thing for which Nathan was envied by all the old men of the village. Every Sunday and on rare occasions when he visited the local pub he wore the finest moleskin waistcoat in the county.

As a drinking man Nathan was at the bottom of the fourth division. Occasionally however he would rapidly promote himself to the top of division one with one almighty thirst.

The Red Fox had been built at the top of a steep rise leading out of the village. Ben Straw, the landlord, calculated that the climb was worth an extra half pint per customer to his takings.

The regulars drank to excess only when there was a special occasion to celebrate.

Lofty Pearce had been placed second to The Major's giant dahlia specimens for eight consecutive years at the annual village show. So when the vicar's goat escaped and dined upon Major Pitchford's exhibition blooms Lofty won the Pitchford Rose

Bowl for best exhibit in show with a weather bleached earwig chewed semi-decorative. Everyone except the Major was delighted and the ale ran freely.

It was during this celebration that Ted Farr blundered through into the snug already belligerently intoxicated. He demanded a pint of bitter to be tagged to his slate. Well aware of the problems Ted could cause when under the influence, Ben ordered him to turn round and get off home.

"I'll turn you round Neb Warts" he bellowed, then realising even in his befuddled state what he had said, held onto the bar and roared with laughter until he collapsed into a convulsing heap on the floor and was dragged outside. From that moment Ben was known throughout the village as Neb.

No-one ever found out why Nathan took both the dog and the pig to the pub that particular Autumn evening. He left them both tethered to the bike on the cobbled forecourt while he drank himself to saturation point.

No-one ever asked him why or how he managed to get the pig into the front carrier or why he decided to set off for home riding his bike.

All went well until he reached the point where the hill swung away to the right, but Nathan the bike and the pig took the line that the crow flies. A heap of gravel in readiness for winter use launched the rider and his passenger into the night air. A sober cyclist would have suffered life threatening injuries at the very least. The gallon of ale slashing around inside Nathan acted as a water bed. Completely unscathed he picked himself up. The pig, stone cold sober was not so lucky, its right front leg was broken.

Back at Latch Cottage the yard broom stale was cut in half and the pieces bound tightly as splints on either side of the pigs leg with yards of old binder-twine.

The sight of a fully grown pig sitting in the front of a carrier bike, its leg stuck out before it like the prow of a ship, being pushed around the village was the funniest thing to happen since the damson tree had fallen and trapped Ted Forrest in his own privy one Saturday night. The church bells had stopped ringing the following morning before anyone heard his cries for help.

Up until the demise of the village school in the early 1960's a casual visitor would have questioned the derivation of a certain ditty accompanying the girls skipping games in the playground.

    Nathan Pegg bought a pig
    He taught that pig to dance a jig

The pig got drunk and so did Pegg
The pig fell down and broke his leg.

On the 9th of May 1957 Nathan Pegg cycled over to the next village where Len Waits had a stone masonry business.

Len read the scruffy piece of paper Nathan shoved into his hands
    HERE LIES PIG
    A GOOD FRIEND
    AGE 21

"Half a crown a letter" he said.

ELI WELCH

Village prosperity mainly depended on the success or failure of the crops. Bitter memories of the depression years still lingered on. Crop and stock prices had dropped to a level where it was difficult to make ends meet.

Work with, not against nature was the first commandment of farmer and small holder.

Eli Welch was the man all workers of the land consulted when a weather forecast was needed. He lived with his wife Mary at Brook Cottage where they had resided since Eli had reluctantly retired at the age of 79.

Now well into his late eighties, he spent most of his days thinking and talking about his life as a shepherd. From the age of twelve he had known no other life. Irrespective of weather, he had spent his days and many nights in the hills. During lambing season an iron wheeled stubble hut, dragged years ago to the head of the valley, became his home, where he lived like a hermit, tending his flock.

He gave every sheep a name and knew every individual. Such was his skill that no other hill flock in the county could match his lambing average.

Some villagers said that the weather did what Eli told it to do, others more rationally that he had lived nearer to it than anyone else.

Most days Eli could be found leaning over the wicket gate to the cottage, a haze of blue smoke rising from a pipe, so stubby that its glow had permanently reddened his nose. His eyes were always set towards the hills watching the moving flecks of white as the sheep grazed.

Eli had forecast the great storm of 1917 five days before it broke. Those that took heed battened down stacks and stock, those that did not spent heavily the following winter. "Will it be a good day to mow the hay tomorrow Eli?" a passer-by would ask. No reply would be offered until Eli had gone through his ritual.

He would draw deeply on his black hickory pipe, blow a cloud of smoke curling into the air and watch until all traces had drifted away. His eyes, shaded under cupped hands would look towards the highest land at all points of the compass. Finally he would take three deep breaths, sucking in the air like a shaft horse pulling up hill "Yup lad" or "leave it for a day or two" came the advice.

As though the concentration had exhausted him, he would then turn and with joints cracking like dead twigs, he would make his way slowly back to the cottage.

The school lads and a few girls liked to find Eli at his cottage gate ready to tell them some strange and wonderful story from his past; an age which they found very difficult to believe ever existed.

One of their favourite stories which Eli had told on many occasions concerned his first trip to a sheep auction.

As a lad of thirteen with a year of full time experience under his belt, Eli had been told to help the master shepherd and his dogs to drove a large flock to market.

Having kept the pace for every step of the twelve miles, matched every move of the men as they shed and split and penned the flock. Eli decided that he was man enough to join in with the traditional adult celebrations at the Three Tuns, before beginning the journey home. Tankards of rough ale flowed in Eli's direction from old drovers, repeating the same cruel joke that had probably been played on them in their youthful years.

Too late, through blurred eyes Eli noticed that the master shepherd had already gone. With night rapidly closing in, Eli on wobbly legs and with a disorientated brain began the long walk home. He moved like a ghost on a maiden visit to a new haunting ground.

Eli never did remember how he got back to Tuttleborough that night. All he knew was that he woke up next morning under a sheet of wrinkly-tin in the garden of a cottage four doors away from his home.

There had been a severe frost that night. Everything was sparkling crystal white in the clear dawn light, except for the rectangle of soil where Eli had slept.
Fearing the wrath of his parents he went straight to work, not returning home until six o'clock that evening.

"Thought you might stay at your Aunt Polly's after that long walk" was all that Mother said. "Knew you wouldn't worry" replied Eli secretly praying that Aunt Polly would not be seen for at least another six months. The following Sunday at chapel Eli signed the pledge as his Father had done before him.

The Widow Ellie

People who live in the neighbouring village of Clugton said they always knew when there had been a death in Tuttleborough because they could hear the silence.

The death of a villager took away an ingredient from their recipe for a unique way of life. No one could live in Tuttleborough without adding their own particular flavour to the community.

The countryman cared little for the town folk's bland description of him as a clodhopping eccentric. The habits of a land worker were often whimsical but more frequently born of necessity than any desire to be odd by choice.

Following a funeral it was the custom for the women at the village store and the men in the Red Fox to reminisce for hours upon the life of the deceased. It was a fond tribute of respect and a final thanks for their contribution to the day to day life of the village.

On November 1st, 1937 Mrs Ellie Norris passed peacefully away at the age of 97.

She was found by Les Titley, the milkman, sitting in her easy chair with Fluff her constant feline companion curled up on her lap. Fluff had also begun his last long sleep.

During a severe attack of bronchitis the previous month Dr. Aston had asked if he could arrange for her to be moved to her eldest daughter's home in the town. Being fiercely independent the widow Ellie had bluntly refused.

"In that case you will have to take extra special care of yourself otherwise you will be following in husband Ron's footsteps" the doctor warned her.

"Hope not" replied Ellie, "I don't think he will have gone in the same direction as I want to go". "In any case what about Fluff, he's been with me for twenty two years, I rescued him from a sack in the brook".

In 1857, at the age of sixteen Ellie had married Ron Norris, the young Waggoner at the estate where she was a domestic. By 1877, twelve babies had been born to Ellie and Ron, five of which had been laid to rest in the church graveyard before their first birthdays.

At the age of thirty seven, Ellie was widowed when Ron fell from the top of a Dutch barn and broke his neck.

Ron's grave was dug next in line to his five offspring. Ellie was left to fend for the remaining seven.

The Manor and the church offered a little help but Mrs Norris vehemently refused anything she considered to be charity.

Visitors to Ellie's cottage would always be offered a bowl of stew from what she called her welcome pot, a huge black cauldron that bubbled and simmered away night and day on the range. It was loaded with some new ingredient almost every day so that its contents never tasted the same on two consecutive days.

On this ever changing strange nameless broth the widow Ellie had raised a healthy family.

In season she gathered violets, primroses and bluebells from the woods, whinberries and heather sprigs from the hills, harvested watercress from the brook, picked blackberries from the hedgerows and stripped the trees of hazel and chestnuts for sale at the market.

Everyone except Jerry Bell, the gamekeeper and the Major knew that Nathan Pegg, the rodent man, had taught Ellie all the tricks of the poacher's art, in exchange for a weekly plug of tobacco.

The gathering of women in the shop spoke of all these things. They remembered Ellie winning best apple pie for five years in succession at the fête. Spoke in admiration of the night Ellie carried her sick child through a snow storm for eight miles to the cottage hospital.

They laughed a little when they recalled the day when Simpson's bull trampled through Ellie's precious vegetable patch and how the beast had been driven off by an irate Ellie belabouring it with an umbrella.

On the morning of the widow Ellie's funeral it was discovered that her grave had not been dug. Four volunteers from the estate began work half an hour before the service. When the bearers carried the coffin to its final resting place, four sweating red faced men rested on their picks and shovels with heads reverently bowed.

Norm Knew His Onions

The village flower show was held at the annual fête on the last Saturday in August.

Norman Wall had just one all consuming interest in his garden which was confined to the vegetable bed. He did not grow a wide range of crops, in fact if there was not a class at the show for a giant exhibit of a particular vegetable, Norm did not waste time on it.

The biggest onion, heaviest marrow, longest runner bean and huge potatoes were the culmination of his season's toil. Rarely did any other exhibitor stand the remotest chance of winning any of these classes. Norm took greatest pride when his onions were placed first. Visitors and villagers alike looked with admiration and a little jealousy at onions nearing the size of footballs, displayed behind a red card bearing Norman's name. No one knew how such mammoth results were achieved. On many occasions Norm had been asked to reveal his secret recipes. Each time he gave what seemed to be a true revelation; but never were two revelations similar.

Would be competitors intent on knocking Norman Wall off his champion's pedestal had once tried to prise the secrets from him after supplying him with a liberal quantity of ale, but to no avail. Undaunted they enlisted the help of Joe Hardy, Norm's next door neighbour. Each evening for a week Joe secretly watched from behind the curtains of his bedroom window, noting every activity Norm carried out on the vegetable plot.

"Nothing unusual" Joe reported back, "Until it's just about to go dark, then he holds his hands high in the air and does a strange kind of dance up and down the rows while muttering some strange incantation. After receiving the news the gang of amateur garden detectives gave up.

During one clement growing season Norm succeeded in growing a specimen onion which for uniformity size and weight surpassed anything that he had previously achieved. It was of such magnificent proportions that he decided to take it on tour.

With the treasured exhibit cosseted in a well lined basket, strapped to his carrier, Norman cycled to four village shows prior to the Tuttleborough event. As expected the giant onion had won four red cards, four rosettes and a silver cup before what was to be its final appearance on home ground.

Between shows the champion exhibit was put on the kitchen window sill each morning to soak up the sunshine, later to be carefully housed in a dark cupboard at night time.

Five days before the big event Norm's wife Molly was rushed into hospital suffering from appendicitis. Molly's sister Martha travelled over to help look after her brother-in-law and two nephews while her sister was away.

Before going to work on the morning of his sister-in-law's arrival, Norm religiously took the onion from its dark hiding place and set it carefully in its usual sun bathing position. At six o'clock that evening Norm returned home after a hard days work at the saw-mill, to be greeted at the kitchen door by a smiling Martha. "Thought I'd cook you a special tea tonight Norman" she said. "Steak and onion. I know it's your favourite, it's all ready. Come and sit down before it spoils!"

GERTRUDE TWIGG

One Tuttleborough parishioner who gave the village an extra dimension over all others was Gertrude Twigg. She was the last of a family who had lived at The Gables for as long as anyone could remember. The house was a large rambling building, showing the scars from years of attack by storm and neglect. It stood in eight acres of land off a minor road leading to Wadbury.

Gertrude's father died a few months after the end of the Great War; since when the land and garden had not been hindered in its rapid return to nature. Her mother had ailed for years with a mysterious illness and was nursed by Gertrude until her death in 1922, thus denying her daughter any chance of romance or marriage.

Left to live alone Gertrude became a recluse. The last time she had been seen in the village was the day of her mother's funeral.

Every Friday evening young Tony Parks, the village errand boy would push the heavy box fronted bike up to The Gables to deliver a week's supplies. He would take back with him money for the goods and a list for the following week's order.

As years went by many rooms in the house became uninhabitable. Eventually Gertrude retreated until finally she had only the kitchen in which to live. The door leading to the interior of the house was crudely boarded up.

The kitchen was a large red tiled room. A huge cooking range imposed itself against one wall; two enormous cupboards entirely concealed another. On the third was a solid Welsh dresser cluttered with a collection of ornaments and cooking utensils. A sturdy elm wood table stood in the middle of the floor accompanied by a solitary ladder backed chair. Gertrude slept on a low collapsible canvas bed with her head under the table and her feet under the sink.

She did not live entirely alone, a small flock of laying hens, a paddle of ducks, a gaggle of geese, cats too numerous to count and a white nanny goat shared the accommodation.

The animals scratched around the unkempt grounds during the day until at the first signs of dusk they would obediently gather outside the kitchen door waiting to be admitted.
Gertrude would open the doors to the two enormous wall cupboards upon which each bird would fly or waddle to its allocated place. The goat would then be tethered to a leg of the table. Each morning her feathered friends would be fed on the kitchen floor while Gertrude had her breakfast.

It could have been this daily routine or Tony's tales of the stench emanating from the house that earned Miss Twigg the nickname "Dirty Gerty".

Village folklore and legend frequently had its beginnings at the occurrence of some unexplained phenomena in the distant past or was created around the eccentricities of the inhabitants.

As Gertrude's self imposed exile from the village continued many fallacious stories circulated around The Gables. The school children in particular used their vivid imaginations to create many fantastic tales concerning poor Miss Twigg.

When youngsters reached school age, the stories would be repeated and embellished until gradually during the passing of years they began to believe in them. Gertrude came near to being a pariah and her house a place so sinister that only the very bravest youngster would walk past it alone. It was said that birds never sung in the gardens at The Gables.

The hunt followers claimed that foxes had re-directed their escape routes to avoid the place.

Flashes of lightening had been seen over the house when there was no sign of a local storm. A series of bright lights had hovered over the estate then slowly descended only to disappear into the house one Halloween night so Tom Bullock said.

From then on the most gullible of children referred to Gertrude Twigg as 'the witch'.

With all vestige of acceptance by the villagers eroded and her character in ruins the events following the sudden disappearance of young Tony Parks the errand boy were predictable.

When Tony had not returned to the shop one hour after his usual arrival time Mrs Lovatt walked down the street to see if he had gone straight home. As he had not, she and Mr Parks retraced the lad's route to eventually find the abandoned delivery bike in the lane leading to the home of Miss Twigg. Only three items of grocery remained in the box. Mrs Lovatt recognised them as Miss Farr's order which would normally have been Tony's last stop. Miss Gertrude Twigg's order had obviously already been delivered.

Together they made their way up the overgrown path to hammer on the door of the house. News of Tony's disappearance had already spread like a heath fire around the village.

When it was reported where the delivery bike had been found Tony's school friends levelled gory accusations against the village witch.

Getting no reply to their banging on the door Mrs Lovatt and Mr Parks hurried back to the village to report the incident to the village policeman. After patiently listening to the details while making a few notes Constable Gwilt mounted his bicycle and set off for the Gables.

Concerned adults and a rabble of youngsters set off in all directions to scour the nearby fields.

The constable returned to tell Mrs Parks that Tony had delivered Miss Twigg's groceries and was seen to begin the return journey with money and next week's order. He had no reason to think that Miss Twigg had spoken other than the truth.

As daylight faded, one by one the search parties returned without finding a single clue as to what had become of Tony.

P.C. Gwilt decided that the situation was serious enough to enlist the help of the county constabulary. He was about to telephone headquarters when a dishevelled figure appeared in he distance, half walking, and half lurching along the lane. With a cry of relief Mrs Parks rushed forward to greet her prodigal son, with all the fussy affection of a broody hen. "Tony where have you been?" she sobbed. "You had us worried out of our minds".

"No-where Mum" Tony replied, his voice coming from purple tinged lips set in an ashen white face. He wobbled, clutched his stomach then vomited far and wide. "The poor lad's ill" said his mother putting a protective and comforting arm around his shoulders. "I've seen enough to know a drunk when I see one" came Nebs voice, in a stage whisper from amongst the gathering of onlookers.

Mr Parks shot forward as if he had been stung by a horse fly. Grabbing his son by the scruff of the neck he propelled him at speed towards the house. "I'll get to the bottom of this in more ways than one" he promised. A couple of days went by before the truth about Tony's brief disappearance was revealed.

Under interrogation by his father Tony had admitted to being drunk. His version of events proudly told to his school mates was a topic of playground conversation for the next fortnight.

Before starting his regular delivery round Tony had borrowed, as he put it, a bottle of his mother's damson wine, intending to play a trick on Miss Twigg. He planned to pour half the bottle into the goat's drinking trough then refill the bottle with water and return it to the larder and no one would be the wiser.

His intention was to watch until the animal started to behave strangely then rush off to tell his pals that the witch had put a spell on the goat. Unfortunately he had tasted the wine first, and finding it much to his liking considered it a terrible waste to feed it to the goat. Instead he found a secluded spot deep inside a wheat field and drank the lot. Four hours later he woke up feeling very peculiar.

It could be said that Miss Gertrude Twigg had the last laugh over the villagers. She left the district. No one saw her go; no one knew where she went to. One day the house stood deserted; it was as if the Tuttleborough witch had spirited herself away. The Gables remained empty, apart from a few brave incursions by children in response to dares, until 1940, when it was commandeered by the army for use as the Home Guard headquarters.

BILLY BUFTON

Just as every royal court once had its jester, every English village once boasted its unfortunate one. No matter to which village they had been assigned they conformed to the same instruction manual.

A cloth cap pulled tight to the brow line topped a chubby round ruddy complexioned face. Irrespective of circumstances a benign smile was an ever present feature. Being unable to read or write was a pre-requisite for the job. Newsprint was a waste of ink while the calculation of height, weight, area or volume was a devious plot laid by the school boss to complicate the life of his pupils. No one however was as adept at mental arithmetic where money was involved. Their gift for knowing automatically that treble nineteen, treble sixteen, double top was a finish from 145 defied explanation! The record time for downing a yard of ale always belonged to them.

All these talents were contained in a body that could have absorbed fifteen rounds of punishment from the world middleweight champion.

Billy Bufton was a member of this elite band. He had no permanent occupation, nor did he wish it. When villagers had a job to do which was either too heavy, boring or downright unsavoury, Billy's help would be sought.

Peggy Whittle had been badgering her husband Ralph to re-lay the uneven stone slabs outside the dairy for many months. After her final threat not to cook roast beef and Yorkshire pudding again until the job was done, Ralph sent for Billy.

Those who had employed him knew that unless the job was explained in detail and he was subjected to initial supervision, he was very likely to turn his attention to some other task he considered to be more important.

Billy arrived at the holding just as Ralph was setting off for the cattle market. He delayed just long enough to explain what was needed to be done.

Happy in the knowledge that his favourite meal by then had been secured, Ralph returned home by mid-afternoon only to find the slabs lying peacefully undisturbed. But the stack yard gate swung easily on its hinges.

A message carried by the twins brought Billy back to the farm the following morning.

His indefatigable smile momentarily faded away when he saw Ralph straining to lift the first slab with a huge crowbar.

"Hi, gaffa you're doing my job" he blurted out, and then stood watching disconsolately. "No, just thought I would get the job started before going up the top field" Ralph replied, applying pressure downwards on the bar.

As the slab lifted he bent swiftly down to scoop something from the earth beneath. "Must be my lucky day Billy, look at that". He held out his hand to reveal a very shiny silver shilling. Quickly popping the coin into his waistcoat pocket Ralph handed the crow bar to Billy and walked away. "Right leave it to me now gaffa, see you later", shouted Billy, tearing off his waistcoat and throwing it to one side.

Mr Whittle paused and looked back towards the dairy. "The fate of my Sunday dinner rests on you Billy", he shouted. "Make sure you do a good job. Oh! And thanks the gate swings beautifully". Billy did not reply; he was working feverishly on the second slab.

When Ralph returned a couple of hours later he found Billy standing like a triumphant war lord in the middle of a perfectly smooth bed of slabs, his smile as wide and bright as a new moon.

"My lucky day as well gaffa", he shouted as Ralph approached. Plunging his hand into his trouser pocket he withdrew a florin and a half crown. "Found this un in the middle and that un at the far end", he beamed. Billy never knew that he had been duped. Ralph was more than happy to pay out the extra to secure his favourite dinner.

As the thirties drew to a close so did the working lives of the Tuttleborough heavy horses. Some were sold, others retired to permanent pasture. Only Bert Walford kept the majestic captain in regular employment. Standing at eighteen hands, when decked in his full set of polished regalia, he was always one of the main attractions at the village fête.

To see teams of draught horses still in daily use one had to travel to three miles over Windle Farm at Wadbury.

Billy had a great love of horses. There had been occasions when he had volunteered to work without pay providing the job involved horses.

Thus it was that Billy would frequently walk over to Clem Morgan at Windle Farm. He always hoped for work but was happy enough even when his luck was out and he only got to feeding or grooming the animals.

Clem did not encourage these visits. He was a man who kept himself very much to himself. He was not fond of conversation which required more than two sentences and hated interruptions when he was working.

One of Billy's irritating habits was to watch a man working then to ply him with questions about what he was doing, why he was doing it and how it was done. Often the same question would be asked half a dozen times. One conversation between Clem and Billy was fondly remembered in the village.

When Billy arrived Clem was hammering away at a huge piece of metal.
"What yer doing Clem?"
"Inventing a flung dingler"
"What's a flung dingler Clem?"
"A machine for flinging dung"
"Why do you need one of them?"
"Saves time carting muck to the fields"
"How does it work Clem?"
"Like a big catapult"
"Good idea Clem, give the osses a rest"
"Tell you what Billy, I'll give you a guinea for every order you get."

Billy went back to the village to spread the good news throughout the farming community.

Only Sam Smart was cruel enough to give Billy a firm order for the revolutionary machine. Realising what Clem had done and not wishing to embarrass Billy further all the other would be customers told him they would wait and see; a well proved maxim of all true county people.

Billy gave up his farm to farm salesmanship when he arrived at Hill Top. Mr Whittle patiently explained to him that a flung dingler would never be any use to a Tuttleborough farmer because the wind always blew from the North. "All we would do is get our own back" explained Ralph.

It was a lovely late summer's day when Billy next visited Windle Farm. Clem was sitting on top of a field gate looking over the year's crop of spring lambs in the sheep creep.

The last person Clem wanted near him when he was culling stock was Billy. He muttered answers to the first three questions then ignored the next half dozen. Suddenly he turned to Billy. "I'm glad you came today Billy, I've got a job for you". "With the osses Clem?" "Yes, Billy with one of the horses. Take Blossom and the flat cart down to the quarry and bring back a load of post holes".

Billy removed his cap then scratched into his mop of rusty hair before thoughtfully moving towards the stable.

"Dafter than I thought" muttered Clem then minutes later as Billy drove the horse and cart out onto the road. When Billy returned more than two hours later Clem was still sorting out his flock. Unconcerned he looked over towards Billy and shouted "Tip them over in the corner of the rickyard". "Right" replied Billy.

Puzzled but not wanting to end this play Clem added "You'd better put some hurdles round 'em to stop anybody falling down 'em". "Don't worry" came back the curt reply. "I've tipped them upside down". Clem did not reply. He suddenly realised that Billy had just spent two hours doing what he enjoyed most. He also had the uneasy feeling that Billy had just reaped a gentle revenge for the flung dingler incident. Billy was not so daft after all.

The Village Concert

When the heroes returned home to the village after the Great War, a service of thanksgiving was held. As a further welcome a dinner was organised in the parish hall, followed by a concert. Ever since that occasion an annual concert held on the last Saturday evening of September had become a tradition. The event was eagerly awaited by adult and child alike. There was never a lack of volunteers to erect a temporary stage, set out rows of chairs or provide a donation towards the refreshments table.

Some of the men had been heard to comment that their women folk saved their best baking performance for concert day. Certainly the traditional wholesome no frills farmhouse cooking would suddenly display a touch of the haute cuisine.

The vicar had taken on the responsibility of gathering together a concert party. Major Pitchford had once held this unenviable position. Some performers had resented being ordered military style to appear on stage but found it difficult to refuse a request by the clergyman. This being so, the same bill of amateur artists appeared year after year, as quite frequently did the same act. It did not deter an audience from turning up or detract from their enjoyment of the evening.

Charlie Groom's first performance as compère had been considered rather earthy by some of the ladies. Subsequently the vicar's blue pencil transformed Charlie into a ladies' favourite, if less appreciated by the men.

The entertainment always began with Hughie Howie giving a short talk on the beauty of the English countryside, illustrated with glass slides projected form his magic lantern. No one else was ever allowed to lay even one finger on the gleaming brass trimmed mahogany box.

Charlie would stand centre stage dressed in pyjamas with matching bowler hat and Wellington boots. In between acts he would tell a few jokes in dead pan Harold Lloyd style.

"Had to go to bed wearing wellies last night, the hot water bottle was leaking".
"One of the hens sat on a golf ball, hatched out an eagle".

The first musical act was always the vicar's wife who would sing either 'Jeannie with the light brown hair' or 'Cherry Ripe', in her untrained slightly squeaky mezzo soprano voice. Her accompanist, Mr Wade the church organist had perfected the art of pressing the loud pedal at exactly the precise moment his soloist fell a few tones flat.

The end of each act would be met with loud enthusiastic applause; arguably in some cases because it had come to an end.

Di Williams was the only man in the village who thought he could play the musical saw, everyone else knew that he could not.

Adults were prepared to tolerate once a year the strange whining sounds Di's vibrating saw produced. The school lads prayed for a repeat of the year when the instrument slipped and Di hurriedly left the stage clutching at blood stained trousers.

Charlie Groom's solo spot was a highlight of the evening, partly because something usually went wrong. He would change his compère's outfit for a battered straw hat sporting a sickle feather from a cockerel, a white milking slop and an enormous pair of boots. The latter he had to borrow from Jim Bugg whose size fourteen feet demanded specially made boots.

Between concerts Charlie would glean snippets of village gossip to weave into verse after verse of the current year's comic song. Each verse was punctuated by a chorus which he sung while performing a comic dance around a cardboard model of the village pump. Occasionally he would forget his words and have to be prompted by the vicar, off stage. Rarely did he hear first time, so would stop and say 'pardon vicar'.

Charlie became a legend in his own life time when in the middle of verse twelve, following an over exuberant stamp of his giant right foot, the stage collapsed. Charlie and the cardboard effigy disappeared amongst the trestle legs. Unperturbed he was dragged out, the stage quickly re-erected and to thunderous applause started from verse one all over again.

A touch of class was added to the programme when Ben Straw with his fine baritone voice led the audience through a selection of songs from the Great War era. Finally the National Anthem was sung and the evening ended when all the food had been appreciatively but rapidly devoured. The children were hurried off home, most of the men walked up the hill to the pub, while the ladies with the vicar's help generally tidied up. Snatches of some of Charlie's verses were heard being sung on the street for a few days after the concert. Like the chorus, they were whimsical, even trite. Nobody cared, it was their song about the village and they were proud of Charlie and his minstrel talent.

During the twenty one year history of the village concert, only two remained indelibly printed on the memory.

The last one of the twenties decade had progressed as planned up to the fourth act. For the first and only time Jerry Bell, the gamekeeper, had been persuaded to appear. He was whistling through his vast repertoire of bird song and had ascended to the Reed Warblers cadenza when Mrs Baris cried out "Oh! No the baby's coming".

There was a sudden hush in the hall, lasting all of three seconds. The youngsters were quickly ushered out; the men disappeared as if by magic, leaving the women to deliver Mrs Baris of a son to join her five daughters.

A few weeks later the unfortunate infant was christened Oliver David. From school days onwards he was always called 'Od'.

Six years later rumour and speculation ran riot through the village during the week leading up to the concert. The vicar had pinned a poster to the Parish Hall door giving details of the programme. The top of the bill read Mystery Guest and the Amazing Mungo.

Some said it was a magic act, others a juggling duo. Most of the school lads hoped that Mungo was a strong man, who could break chains and lift a hundredweight sack of corn in his teeth. Mrs Lovatt asked the fat lady in the market who sold pork pies and always knew everything, except on that occasion she did not.

Even Constance and Prudence Midge's curiosity got the better of them and they attended a village concert for the first time.

All the well known entertainers were applauded with the usual enthusiasm. As Charlie came to introduce the mystery guest there was a buzz of excitement in the hall. The curtains opened. A gasp came from the audience, followed by a burst of muted chatter, then a sudden silence.

Standing centre stage dressed in a seaman's uniform was a huge bearded man, with a wide eyed little monkey seated upon his shoulder. A table had been placed on stage carrying an assortment of props.
"I am midshipman Morgan, let me introduce you to my friend the amazing Mungo", he said in a broad lilting unrecognisable accent.
"I rescued him from a trader in Mombassa; he understands every word I say" "Mungo jump onto the table"

Mungo did not move a muscle, not even to blink. "Come on Mungo, quick now onto the table". Midshipman Morgan commanded in a stern authoritative voice. Mungo clasped his paws over his eyes; a ripple of embarrassed laughter greeted his reaction.

"He's probably got a bit of stage fright" offered Morgan visibly showing signs of irritation. "Here Mungo catch", the sailor tossed an orange into the air.

Mungo remained motionless on his master's shoulder. The orange fell splat onto the stage.

No one knew whether they were watching a comedy act and were supposed to laugh, or whether the poor monkey was just too scared to move.

"He just can't resist peanuts", blustered Morgan taking a handful from his pocket and holding them at arm's length.

At last the obstinate Mungo made a move, but not the one that was scheduled. He leapt from the sailor's shoulder, landed briefly on the outstretched hand, then with one huge bound into the centre isle of the hall.

If the intruder had been a pugnacious game cock, a savage dog or a runaway horse, everyone would have known what to do, but an escaped monkey was completely out of their world of experience.

Frantic shouts of "sit still, don't frighten him" from Morgan went unheeded. The women shrieked, the youngsters scattered while some of the men made crude lunges in an attempt to capture the escapee.

Mungo nimbly outwitted them all by scaling a curtain then swinging from one ceiling strut to another before disappearing through an open window.

Led by a demoralised midshipman Morgan, some of the men, followed at a safe distance by a ragtaggle of boys set out on a search. It was not long before they realised that to find a monkey in the dark, with so many tall trees in the vicinity was a waste of time. Everyone except Morgan returned to the hall for the refreshments. There was only one topic of conversation but many suggestions as to who midshipmen Morgan was and to where his monkey might have gone.

The following morning only Billy Bufton and half a dozen of the Spragg family were available to help Morgan in his unsuccessful search.

On Monday morning a boldly written card was displayed in the window of the village store. 'Ten shillings reward for information leading to the capture of Mungo', it read.

The search was on. Every girl and boy scanned trees, peered into hedgerows and tramped the fields before and after school hours in the hope of claiming the generous reward money.

By the following Thursday, even the most persistent searcher had to reluctantly admit that Mungo would probably be miles away, on his way back to Africa.

In the very early hours of Friday Mrs Lovatt was awoken from her sleep above the shop by strange sounds coming from below. Armed with a warming pan and a torch she crept downstairs. The beam fell on the intruder, sitting on top of the counter amidst the remains of half eaten fruit, a bag of spilt raisins and numerous broken biscuits.

Cans and cartons had been unceremoniously dumped on a floor from which sugar crystals glistened in a carpet of flour.

The village constable arrived at the shop and was then seen to cycle over to the vicarage.

Well before shop opening hours a car drew up outside. A passenger emerged carrying a wicker basket and entered the shop. A few minutes later the car, driver, passenger and wicker basket were heading out of Tuttleborough.

Mrs Lovatt told her many customers that morning about the reward and the extra pound note she got for all the damaged goods.

The vicar never did reveal who midshipman Morgan was or where he came from.

Weeks later the fat lady at the market, who sold pork pies and knew everything, told Mrs Culshaw, the blacksmith's wife that she remembered a brother of Rev. Sequera's wife who had run away to sea many years ago.

A Royal Fête

On Wednesday May 12th, 1937 Tuttleborough joined the whole nation in celebration of the Coronation of King George VI and Queen Elizabeth.

A few weeks previously Major Pitchford had called together the village show and fête committee. For such an auspicious occasion it was decided to substitute some of the traditional attractions such as 'flinging the dead rat' and 'downing a yard of ale' with events more suited to the celebration of a royal occasion. Thus it was agreed to introduce a bonny baby competition and an inter-village tug-of-war contest for which the Major promised to donate a special Coronation Cup to the winning team. The produce, handicrafts and flower show would be limited to parishioners, with sports and rural activities open to all comers.

The chosen site for the festivities was a ten acre rough pasture field known locally as 'The Bottoms'. A sluggish meandering brook cut the field roughly in half; access to either side was over a single plank footbridge.

From early morning of the great day activity on the field was frenetic.

Two large off-white tents loaned by the brewery had been erected. The flower show tent stood proudly square but the beer tent for some unaccountable reason had a list of at least ten degrees to the right. In the eyes of most of the men it would probably have righted itself by late afternoon.

As the church clock struck two, the Major introduced Lady Cynthia to the gathering of eager villagers.

Wearing a long white satin dress with matching scarlet gloves and ostentatiously wide brimmed hat, she was helped up to stand on an upturned zinc bath thoughtfully draped with an old horse blanket.

"I am honoured to be invited to open your quaint little fête" she said in a voice which conveyed the thought that it was the last place she really wanted to be.

No one seemed to know who Lady Cynthia was. The fat lady from the market who sold the pork pies had not yet arrived. As she pronounced the fête open, Aggie Spragg was heard to stage whisper "if she was a real lady she wouldn't be 'ere she'd be at the abbey".

Lady Cynthia's other duty was to judge the bonniest baby competition.

Eleven youngsters had been spruced up in their frilliest dresses. The bald, the hairy, the crying, the gurgling, the chubby, the scrawny, each one the apple of their mother's eye, were given the same treatment. A tickle under the chin form a scarlet gloved hand, a few unintelligible garbled baby noises, a condescending smile to the proud mother, then everyone waited to see to which perambulator Lady Cynthia would attach the red rosette.

The baby carriages began to fade away into the field as young Michael Stant from Clugton was awarded a title he would not be too keen to boast about in five years' time.

Mr Leese the school boss organised the children's sports with his usual efficiency and discipline. The Spragg twins easily won the three legged race simply because they tied their ankles together with a piece of knicker elastic. The sack race had to be re-run after Phil Anker's feet were seen to be sticking out of strategically placed holes.

All competitors were presented with a bag of Winnie Harvey's home made treacle toffee. This was guaranteed to glue their jaws together and keep them quiet for at least half an hour.

The slow bicycle race was as usual a foregone conclusion. On the signal of 'go' all the competitors except for P.C. Gwilt moved very slowly forward. The constable turned his handlebars to an angle of forty five degrees, locked his feet on the pedals and sat motionless, waiting for everyone else to fall off, then he nonchalantly rode to the finish line.

The judging in the show tent had been completed by mid afternoon with most of the red cards going to the expected winners. The only decision to raise a few eyebrows was the winning entry in the children's pet competition. The talking budgie, the kissing gold fish or even the rather smelly polecat ferret would have been acceptable, but a virtually invisible stick insect on a sprig of privet in a two pound jam jar promoted a few adverse comments. Fortunately for Peter Timms the judge had not opened the jar, otherwise he would have discovered that the winner was dead and had been glued to its perch.

The two most eagerly awaited events were scheduled to take place at the end of the afternoon. The entrants for the mile long obstacle race changed in the beer tent to emerge wearing a strange assortment of long shorts and unfamiliar running pumps. Dave Jones had won the last two races beating Reg Casewell, his great rival by a few yards on both occasions. It was well known that Dave was very keen to complete a hat trick of victories. It was also rumoured that Reg had indulged in a special training programme. Certainly he had not been seen up at the Red Fox for at least a month. This was to be a crunch meeting and expectations for a great race were high.

Fifteen runners set off, by the end of the first circuit, ten remained. As the third and final lap began only six serious contenders were left to fight it out. Dave and Reg had shadowed each other every step of the way, never moving more than a yard away from each other. As the rest of the field tailed off the two protagonists approached the penultimate obstacle with only the width of a blade of grass between them. They had only the flat bed drey to overcome and it would be a sprint over the foot bridge to the finish. Dave leapt for the drey a few yards in the lead. Reg seizing the opportunity in both hands grabbed hold of Dave's shirt, dragged him back, and then hoisted himself over the obstacle and on to victory.

Some spectators clapped and cheered his audacity; others booed and jeered such an act of ungentlemanly conduct. Dave Jones said nothing. Victory to him at next year's fête would be all the sweeter.

Four teams had entered the Coronation Cup tug-of-war competition. Tuttleborough the hosts, Clugton the natural enemy, a team of unknown potential from Wadberry and a scratch group of strong hard drinking drovers from the cattle auction.

To everyone's great delight Clugton were drawn to pull against Wadberry first, leaving Tuttleborough versus the drovers; the winners from the first round to contest a best of three pull final. To add to the enjoyment of the occasion it had been decided to stage the contest across the narrow neck of the brook. A team would be deemed the winner when any of the opposing side ended up with a ducking.

The men of Wadbury were no match for Clugton. Hardly had the command 'pull' been given before the first three men had taken a very early if dirty bath.

The home team and the drovers was a more evenly matched affair. First one team then the other were brought to the brink of defeat. Urged on by a fiercely partisan crowd ably led by the extremist Aggie Spragg, the Tuttleborough eight, after minutes of dead lock, responded to the crowd's encouragement. With one last gut-busting effort all resistance from the drovers evaporated. Six of them lay gasping for breath on the bank while two very soggy individuals were dragged out of the brook.

Tuttleborough had earned their passage into the final the hard way. Clugton men had hardly shed a bead of perspiration between them.

Despite a protest from the Clugton coach, it was agreed to have a fifteen minutes recess before the grand final. The pride of two villages was at stake. Neither team could contemplate defeat, particularly at the hands of the traditional enemy.

A nerve tingling silence fell as the combatants took the strain for the first pull. Not an inch of ground was given by two evenly matched teams. With muscles bulging, faces reddening and grunts increasing in volume, it seemed that a gentleman's agreement on an honourable stale mate was imminent, when anchor man Jim Bugg's size fourteen boots slipped. The Clugton coach seized upon the opportunity and the home team slithered on their backsides to a one nil deficit.

Initial groans of despair quickly followed by words of encouragement rippled round the crowd.

A short breather, a change of ends, more spitting on hands and the contest was alive again. The Clugmen arrogantly settled into position expecting a quick two leg victory. They had actually dispensed with the time honoured hand lubricant. They had badly miscalculated the measure of Tuttleborough determination and pride. For fully five minutes every sinew strained and very slowly as a hundred or so unqualified coaches screamed pull! Pull! The indomitable home team drew level at one leg each.

Even football matches between the two villages had not aroused such fervid passions.

Sensing victory the home supporters roared their heroes on; but even as the team bent to lift the rope for the final time, disaster struck. The luckless Jim Bugg set solid, his back locked in the ungainly position of an inverted U. Sympathetic hands bowled Jim off and engaged in a private tug-of-war contest in an effort to straighten him out.

The situation became tense. Clugton refused to pull against a seven man team, saying they would not have Tuttleborough claiming that they lost only because they were a man short. After much verbal confrontation the visitors agreed to allow a substitute to take Jim's place.

As Sid Jacks stepped forward he was unceremoniously brushed aside by the wobbling bulk of Aggie Spragg. "You can go back home and tell them you were beaten by a team with a woman in it" she jibed.

To roars of bemused approval from the onlookers, Aggie picked up the rope's end, wound it purposefully around her enormous girth, planted her clog shod feet firmly on the ground and was ready to sacrifice every ounce of her twenty plus stone for the reputation of the village.

A contest of Leviathan might ensued; spurred on by what they considered to be an insult; Clugton welded their combined efforts to a force which exerted the last drop of human endeavour.

Tuttleborough steadfastly rode the storm. Not an inch of ground was surrendered by either side. No one could have predicted the final outcome of such an evenly matched contest.

The Tuttleborough coach Bill Roberts was watching the opposition like a stoat setting a rabbit, ready to pounce at the first glimmer of relaxation; when suddenly one of the home team broke wind at a magnitude capable of cleaning chaff from a barn.

All resistance from Clugton dissipated and they were dragged laughing and bemused into the brook.

Some people said it was Billy. A few of the team seemed about to sheepishly admit that they had dropped the secret weapon. Those viewing from the anchor end of the rope were in no doubt as to who was responsible for the great and glorious victory. A protest was lodged, but as the Major pointed out, the rules governing tug-of-war make no allowances for the natural functions of the body.

Never had a village fête heard such rejoicing as the moment when Aggie Spragg was presented with The Coronation Cup.

THE FEUD

The feud between the Yapp and Addis families began at a time when hedgehogs could pause to admire their reflection in a puddle while crossing the road; and not fear for their lives.

The village folklore told a story of the time that Ned Addis had bought a horse from Ted Yapp.

Two days later the horse caught the croup Ned said he wanted his money back, but Ted refused saying that he had a horse once that caught the croup.

Ned demanded to know what treatment Ted had given the sick horse. Turpentine was the reply. Ned returned home and immediately gave the sick animal a liberal dose.
The following morning the horse was dead.
Ned rushed back to Ted Yapp's place.
"You told me you gave turpentine to that horse of yours that had the croup" he screamed purple with rage. "I did the same and the damn thing died".
"Ah! so did mine" said Ted sagely.

It was said that Ned in his will demanded to be cremated, so that he would not have to lie in the same graveyard as Ted.

From that day on all conversation between the two families ceased. Three generations later the feud lived on.

A Yapp and an Addis never walked on the same side of the road.

The village store was vacated by a Yapp if an Addis entered.

The school master never dared allow a member of either family to sit together.

If an Addis was drinking in the snug a Yapp drank in the tap room.

Attempts to mediate by three consecutive clergymen had failed abysmally.

The Reverend Sequera had invited both families to share tea with him at the vicarage. Mrs Yapp had bluntly refused. Mrs Addis turned up but stated she would not stay; she would just take her tea home in a bag.

In 1921 the village football team lost one nil to Clugton the mortal enemy, all because Vin Addis crashed a back pass into his own net, leaving the goal keeper Dick Yapp, speechless with anger.

During the Spring of 1936, despite the history of their family backgrounds Maggie Addis and Ron Yapp discovered that they were attracted to each other.

Their courtship road was strewn with pot holes and the occasional deep ravine.

Clandestine meetings were arranged well away from the village, usually only after night fall.

All went well for a week or two until Mrs Addis found a heart with the initials MA and RY entwined at its centre, scratched on the back of the privy door.

Maggie was banned from ever seeing Ron again with the threat that she would be sent away to live with her Aunt Freda if she did.

The days when Maggie's Aunt Freda lived in the village, people thought were best forgotten.

A religious zealot she would deliver long vitriolic sermons to anyone who was absent from Sunday service.

After a brief recess the courtship continued when Ron found that he could shin up a drainpipe and balance on the roof of the lean-to coal shed beneath Maggie's bedroom window.

No one knew how Mr Addis found out about the deception. Ron discovered that he had, when a thick coating of cart grease shot him off the roof like dung from a tumbrel.

In 1939 Ron joined the army. Two years later Maggie moved from the village to work in a munitions factory somewhere near Birmingham.

Their next appearance in Tuttleborough was not until 1945.

Mr & Mrs Ron Yapp had returned to introduce the twins to their grandparents,

English villages were never the same again after the Second World War, but in the case of one it took a war to end a feud that had resisted all other means.

ONE ARM JACK

The gardener at the manor was 'one arm Jack'. His other arm had been left behind in Flanders.

The Major had retained Jack's services upon his return. He rather liked the favourable comments made about him, for so doing, by the villagers.

The missing arm had been replaced by a fearsome looking hook, the sight of which sent youngsters scurrying behind their mother's skirts.

Jack had two claims to village fame. His record distance for hurling a cowpat ninety eight feet nine and three quarter inches at the 1913 fête had never been broken. By 1927 his supreme effort was destined to stand for all time, when the committee substituted the ancient rural art of cow dung hurling with flinging the dead rat.

The vicar as chairman of the fête committee had insisted upon the change following an unfortunate incident the previous year involving the Major's wife who inadvertently had a brief fitting for a new natural hat. It would not have been so serious or so embarrassingly funny if Bob Gregorie's chosen missile had been allowed to dry out in the sun for another day or two.

Jack stubbornly refused to compete in the new event probably because he was a proud man, and no self respecting villager would be seen in public hurling an old sock full of dried peas tied up with a string to form a tail, when Nathan Pegg could have supplied all the dead rats that were needed.

Jack's second claim was as contentious as it was mysterious. From the day of his return from the war after a long convalescence Jack refused to speak. Not one word did he utter to anyone at any time even under extreme provocation.

The community was mystified as prior to Jack's response to Lord Kitchener's request he had been the villagers most verbose character. His coarse rural expletives could set a damp bonfire alight.

Taunts such as tin man, rusty man, and Captain Hook hurled at him from a safe distance by cowardly young lads went unheeded.

Some adults were known to have accidentally bumped into him, on the safe side, to see if their abject apologies would be acknowledged, but they never were.

During the first few months, claim and counter claim was made by some locals swearing that they had heard Jack speak, but as no one could ever substantiate such claims they were dismissed.

Mrs Kinsey at the village store assured everyone that Jack had no need to speak to her because he only ever bought a plug of thick twist. The landlord at The Red Fox had a pewter tankard charged with ale by 8 p.m. every Saturday in readiness for Jack's weekly visit. Four pence would change hands in silence. Men who had changed their drinking hours watched and listened intently in the hope of hearing just one single word of thanks.

Reluctantly they finally admitted defeat so turned their interest towards suggesting reasons for Jacks mute state.

Billy's dad reckoned that Jack had been captured and refused to talk under interrogation, so the hun had chopped off his arm. Having won the contest with silence, Jack had decided never to speak again.

The fat lady in he market who sold pork pies and knew everything, mother of the fat lady who still sat in the market selling pork pies and was reported to know everything said that Jacks loss of voice was caused by eating bully beef and it would never have happened if she could have sent her pork pies over to the boys in the trenches.

The schoolmaster said it was psychosomatic of a physiological disorder caused by the horrendous experience of war which manifested itself in deep trauma.

The villagers listened to his learned explanation intently then told him he was talking a load of bull and that Jack's condition was simply caused by all the bloody horrible things he had been through in France.

Year after year one arm Jack remained stoically silent. The next generation of children asked no questions, believing him to be dumb.

Jack continued to work for the Major and to make his weekly trip to The Red Fox, until the early spring of 1934.

At closing time one Saturday Neb noticed that Jack was sitting motionless in his chair, the pewter tankard untouched on the bar. Jack had passed silently away.

The unenviable task of informing Mrs Anslow of her husband's sad demise fell as usual to Constable Gwilt. In response to his knock at the cottage door, a head appeared at the open bedroom window. She refused his request to speak together inside, demanding to know what he wanted so late at night.

"I'm sorry to be the one to bring you bad news Mrs Anslow" he called up in a loud whisper, "But I'm afraid your husband Jack passed away in The Red Fox tonight."

There was a long awkward silence before Mrs Anslow said coldly "How do you know he's dead?". This was the positive proof that Jack had remained silent even within the privacy of his own home.

The cortege was led by Jacks wife and her five sons, Matthew, Mark, Luke, John and Fred. Jack's secret was laid to rest with him or so it seemed.

An article in the local newspaper in 1940 read 'Private Fred Anslow had good reason to celebrate November 11th. Not only was it his 21st birthday, he was also mentioned in dispatches following selfless action beyond the call of duty, under heavy enemy fire, while serving with his infantry division in France'.

The village lads read and felt very proud. The older men fondly recalled memories of old 'one arm Jack' Fred's dad.

The older women gathered together in the village store. They suddenly remembered Mrs Anslow going away to some unpronounceable place in Wales to look after her sick sister so she said. At the time Jack had been away at war for six months.

When she returned with her new son Fred almost a year later they questioned the fact that the baby looked a lot younger than his mother said he was.

"They don't thrive in that Welsh air" was her only explanation.

Twenty one years later the old women in the village shop just shook their heads knowingly.

A CASE OF BLACK AND WHITE

For six days of the week Constance and Prudence Midge wore black. Only on the Sabbath did they trim their sinister attire. To their bo-peep hats they added white ribbon and wore neat lace apronettes in front of their long drab skirts.

No one knew from whence they came when they moved into the village during the winter of 1930. Rumour was rife.

Aggie Windle said they had worked for royalty and claimed it must be true because she had been told this by the fat lady who sold pork pies at the market, and she always knew everything.

Lettice Benson claimed they had been spreading the good book amongst cannibal tribes on the Dark Continent, but had returned home and become vegetarians. Certainly no one had ever seen them enter the butchers shop.

The custom of all English villages is not to accept newcomers until their tombstone is erected in the grave yard.

To the villagers, the Midge sisters were enigmas; a puzzle they could not solve, a mystery that could not be unravelled.
Such were the feelings in the community during the early months, that the spinster Miss Culshaw had actually approached

the Rev. Sequera to ask if he could exorcise them as one did with poltergeists.

The much maligned sisters remained prim, proper, punctilious and stoically pious.
They would return the casual rare greeting with a slight lifting of the chin and an almost inaudible sniff.

Any villager without a watch could calculate their day by Midge time.

Monday 6 a.m. smoke would begin to rise from the wash-house chimney. 8 a.m. rhythmic movement of the dollypeg could be viewed through the open door way. 9.a.m. the squelch and squeaks of a mangle could be heard. 10 a.m. the washing line was a fluttering study in black and white but never was an under garment displayed by 3 p.m. the line was cleared by 4.p.m. a sedate stroll through the village, a circuit of the church yard before returning home.
Each day had it's own measured recipe. Come Sunday morning with one accord the first chime of the church bell would synchronise with the lifting of the wicket latch.

Dan Pikes holding was situated at the bottom of the long winding rutted cart track. Dan's wife Connie spent her time feeding the hens, ducks, geese, goat, pigs, rabbits, turkeys, guinea fowl, cats, dogs and an adopted one legged stray racing pigeon. A much easier job she claimed then feeding Dan and their growing twin sons Tom and Eric.

To fill the gaps in her week she would bake, scrub, dust, black lead the range, knit, darn, wash the cloths and produce an abundance of farmhouse cheese and butter after hours of separating and churning.

A humped back bridge carried the cart track over a languid turbid stream on the approaches to the stack yard. Every Friday afternoon at precisely ten minutes to three Constance and Prudence Midge struggled through the ill fitting gate to Dan's stack yard on their way to buy a pound of cheese, half a pound of butter and a dozen eggs. To get to the dairy they had to pass the open fronted tackle shed where stood the buck rake, binder, a miscellany of ageing farm tools and a slat sided dray. The floor was a thick carpet of musty hay, swaths of prickly straw and a liberal scattering of dusty chaff.

This was the magic playground for imaginative children and the perfect nesting place for the flock of multi-coloured fowl that strutted around the farmstead.

On one never to be forgotten Friday, unknown to the pious sisters every movement of their visit was been keenly watched by the twins. From the secrecy of the horse drey Tom and Eric drew a bead along the rough edge of the pieces of two by two and exerted gently pressure on the rusty nails hammered into the lower edge. The invaders were about to be repelled. The lethal bullets were never released. The twins' eyes met in astonishment then turned to watch the actions of the two black clad intruders. Their task accomplished the sisters continued on to the dairy to purchase the goods. On the return journey they paused for a moment outside the tackle shed before negotiating the rickety gate and disappeared from the twins view on the far side of the bridge.

Breathless with excitement and babbling incoherently the twins burst into the dairy to tell their mother what they had seen take place in he tackle shed. "My my" was all she replied "I wonder what dad will do about that?"

During breakfast time on the following Friday Dan instructed his sons to clear all the eggs from the shed, then to replace them with any they could find amongst the tangle of weeds at the far end of the yard. As requested the boys diligently scrubbed the foundling eggs clean until one burst where upon Mum had to take over while the absconders ran around the kitchen holding their noses, shouting "poo what a stink".

Being creatures of habit the two sisters upon their arrival, gave an exact repeat performance of the previous Friday. Constance carried a wicker basket upon her arm. On reaching the tackle shed another basket was deftly retrieved from beneath the long black coat of her sister Prudence. It was swiftly filled with eggs then hidden under a pile of straw, to be collected on the return journey. Another week of rural time sauntered by before the thieves' next visit.

The time it took them to walk from the gate to the dairy broke all records. Knowing that the weekly order never varied, conversation had always been irrelevant between Mrs Pike and the Midge sisters. Nevertheless Connie was not really surprised when Constance enquired as to whether the hens feed had been changed. "No! I don't think so; they glean most of it", Mrs Pike replied. "Why do you ask?" "Well" said Constance. Those eggs we had last week, there was something odd about them. In fact if we hadn't have scrambled them I don't think we could have eaten them."

AUNT ALICE

Extending to an area of thirty one and a half acres, Bracken Ridge was the biggest holding in the parish.

It had passed down from father to son down four generations, it was now owned by Bert Walford. He was the only smallholder in the district who managed to support his wife and family entirely from the land.

Bert had married late in life; he would more likely than not have remained a bachelor if he had not been attacked by an irate swarm of bees while hedge brushing. The resultant injuries necessitated a few days in the cottage hospital where he met Elizabeth. Three months later she exchanged her maiden name for Walford, her uniform for an apron and her shift work for a seven day a week sixteen hour a day job. To make up for lost time Bert and Elizabeth had increased the local population by four, two sons and two daughters during the first six years of marriage.

Elizabeth had no previous experience of rural life so brought a rare spontaneity to the arduous regimented routine demanded of a farmer's wife.

While many of the village wives attacked each day as though they were breaching a thorn hedge, Bert's wife smiled through six cooked breakfasts every morning, six wholesome meals each evening and the preparation of a beavy bag five days a week. The same enthusiasm for life was brought to her weekly chores, she seemed to enjoy washing, ironing, scrubbing, dusting and all the other dozens of mundane things it was necessary for her to do.

During the weekdays no family worked harder to succeed than the Walfords. Sunday however, had a unique character of its own. A lie-in meant that breakfast did not send its mouth-watering aroma from sizzling bacon drifting to the black beamed ceiling until eight o'clock. Three hours later the cows had been milked, the stock fed and the family, with the exception of mother, were dressed in their Sunday best. Mother would still be cheerfully nursing the bubbling pans and crackling roasting tins in and around the kitchen range.

Throughout Spring and Summer Bracken Ridge entertained a Sunday guest. Aunt Alice always arrived punctually at two o'clock riding an old tandem bike. She would leave it propped against a cart wheel before entering the tackle shed to step up into the potato scales. No matter how she adjusted the weights they never recorded a reading of less than eighteen stone.

Bert's standing joke about his sister was that baby Sarah was once lost for a fortnight after sitting on Alice's lap.

Aunt Alice was the live-in housekeeper for Major General Kinsey whose huge gaunt house overlooked a village eight miles south of Tuttleborough. One of her many duties was to take the Major General on constitutional tandem rides twice a week. The only complaint she had was the fact that her passenger only pedalled when they were travelling down hill. The only complaint the major general had was that when riding at the rear his view of the countryside was completely obscured.

The children loved their Aunt Alice. She had an infectious jest for life which was immediately transmitted to anyone in her presence.

The afternoon was spent by taking a leisurely walk around the fields. Bert cast an experienced eye over the state of his land and planned his work schedule for the coming week. The children searched for any wild flower or creature they had not found before. Mrs Walford and her sister-in-law caught up with all the village news.

Sunday tea was the only meal of the week that was taken in the front parlour; it never varied. A huge plate of wafer thin sandwiches cut with mathematical precision, buttered scones, a fruit cake, and rich to the point of being black and a shimmering bowl of red jelly made a weekly appearance.

While the majority of the villagers worshipped at the parish church, Bert's family accompanied by Alice joined the congregation at the Primitive Methodist chapel. Only the Tonks household, Neb Straw and Nathan Pegg were regular none attendees at either. If the Rev. Sequera had not got the twins names mixed up at their christening it was likely that Sid and May Tonks would also have attended St. Marks. But if anyone upset the volatile Mrs Tonks they were never forgiven.

Mrs Mitchell" she said, "You go on, I'll catch up with you". Mrs Mitchell was the fictitious lady who lived in the red tin hut beneath the damson plantation.

By the time the family had reached the chapel and settled into the family pew, there was no sign of Aunt Alice.

The air in the chapel was always cold irrespective of season. A squat ugly donkey stove off set from the centre isle puffed wisps of smoke out when the wind blew from the north west combined with the heavy scent of mansion polish, created a heady fug.

The bench pews had been constructed from the hardest wood procurable. More often than not as Mr Pointon, the superintendent and organist played the first chord on the wheezy harmonium; a family of mice would make their escape towards the vestry door. At such times every child and even a few adults would stifle a laugh, bury their faces in a handkerchief and emit bogus coughs.

It was considered a mortal sin to whisper, smile or even twitch particularly during the long long sermons.

The widow Mrs Newns sat in the pew behind the Walfords disconcertingly munching through a crackling bag of crunchy sweets. People still remembered the days when one arm Jack would fall asleep during the sermon, only to be rudely awakened by a savage dig in the ribs from his wife, at the first sound of a snore. There would have been fewer disturbances to the service if she had ignored him. Invariably Jack would wake with a violent jolt, emit a rasping grunt then loose control of his artificial limb sending the metal hook crashing into the seat.

The hymn singing was fervent and melodious, the sound carried as far as Pinfold Cottage where the Tonks family lived, a hundred yards down the road.

From his place in the back pew Walter Swain's fine tenor voice soared above the congregation. Unfortunately Walter had never learned to read, so after the first verse of every hymn, which he had memorised, he used his rare ability to spontaneously make up new words for each succeeding verse.

The most loquacious of all the visiting lay preachers was Mr Tricket. His sermon that evening was a forty minute berating against those that hoarded up material wealth in preference to spiritual salvation: A most inappropriate text where the majority of his congregation could only afford to send their children to school on a breakfast of bread and dripping.

Feeling thoroughly chastised the congregation arose stiff limbed at eight o'clock. By the time Mr Tricket had shook hands with his entire congregation, Aunt Alice had not made an appearance.

"She must be unwell" suggested Elizabeth as the Walford's hurried home. More likely she didn't want to come in late thought Bert.

As they reached the stack yard gate Liz grabbed Bert's arm "listen" she said. Plaintive cries were coming from the privy. "Stay there", Liz ordered, as she rushed off towards the damson trees.

Aunt Alice's bulk determined her method of entry into the privy. Upon unlatching the door, in order to be facing in the right direction she had to enter in reverse. Unfortunately she had slipped, fallen, twisted her ankle and got wedged solid.

With the help of the children Bert managed to gather together a rescue party of half a dozen strong men from he village. After the initial outburst of belly laughs and a few good natured earthy comments their combined efforts prised the unfortunate Alice from her temporary prison; before laying her prostrate on the bacon curing board and staggering towards the house.

Alice eased herself up on one elbow "What hymns did you sing tonight?" she asked, turning towards Liz. 'Lead kindly Light', 'Fight the Good Fight', 'Onward Christian soldiers', can't think of the other one", why do you ask?" enquired Liz

"Oh dear I didn't get one of them right" sighed Alice.

WILF'S GIFT

The parish boundary cut through Wilf Law's garden. Wilf enjoyed telling people that he slept in Tuttleborough but went to the lavatory in Clugton. He used subtle adjustments to his terminology according to whom he was speaking.

Many years ago a Clugton resident had welshed on a debt owed to Wilf. Since that time he had obstinately refused to have anything to do with Clugites as he called them. He would even add four miles into a journey into town simply to avoid passing through the village he utterly condemned.

Wilf was a jack of all trades handyman. The great difference between Wilf and Billy was that he looked for work most of the time where as Billy only worked when he had to. If anyone had ever taken the time to do a few basic calculations it would probably have been discovered that Wilf's casual approach to employment earned him twice as much as a regularly employed agricultural worker. He punctuated his building, walling, hedging, and thatching even bicycle repair skills with seasonal work in the harvest fields.

From generation to generation rural know how and skills had been handed down form mother to daughter and father to son.

Most young lads could set an eel line, tickle a trout and take an average of three rabbits from four snares. Their sisters were adept with cooking pans and knitting needles. Only the mystique of medical remedies from the fields and hedgerows was alas an art now known only to a few of the older women.

Wilf Law had been given a very special talent. To look at him he was anything but out of the ordinary. He was barely five feet tall, thin and wiry, his legs as bandy as a ploughman's. A shock of wired red coarse hair crowned a gaunt red face tinged with a splash of purple on the cheeks. A pair of eyes as blue as corncockle, shone from beneath hooded brows; it was from within those piercing eyes that the villagers said Wilf's talent lay.

As a boy Wilf gained a fine reputation for skilfully nursing injured creatures back to fitness. He frequently had to bravely suffer the punishment doled out for being late at school after spoon feeding a baby hedgehog or matchstick splinting a birds broken leg.

Wilf's mother tolerated the sharing of her house with wild waifs and strays until the week when in quick succession three unfortunate mishaps occurred.

A semi-tame red squirrel, reared from a few weeks old abandoned youngster, escaped secretly into the front room where after tearing the net curtains to shreds, set about disgorging the leather bound settee of its kapok stuffing. The next day a jackdaw (the only bird in the village which flew with a limp after Wilf's orthopaedic skills on a broken wing) landed on the middle of three freshly baked loaves of bread. It part devoured the one in front of it, the one at the back was unorthodoxly christened. All creatures were banished to the outbuildings when a grass snake Wilf had managed to hide in the glory hole under the stairs for two days got away. Wilf's mother had a pathological fear of snakes, so nearly died of apoplexy when she found it nestling amongst a handful of firewood she had taken from the stick box.

Wilf's concern for animals rapidly developed into an uncanny ability to control even the most wayward of domestic beasts. Skittish horses, temperamental cattle, even fearsome boars would return home completely transformed characters after a short period of time under Wilf's influence.

Ever since the Rev. Sequera had returned home from a visit to the cattle auction with a huge mongrel dog named Adolph, only Wilf had been able to safely visit the vicarage, if the beast was on the loose.

The vicar sincerely believed that a change of name, kindness, good food and prayer would convert the most fiendish canine Tuttleborough had ever seen, into a benign lap dog. The rechristened Angel was probably a monstrous genetic mistake. Beneath a thick mat of grizzled grey hair rippled a massively muscular body. His mop sized paws supported long thick set legs. A well furnished tail stuck out behind him at a barber's pole angle. Ears that permanently twitched stood like antennae above a hooded pair of sunken gleaming copper coloured eyes. Yellow fangs stuck out spike like from vice strong jaws. Stalactites of slobber dripped continuously from drooping jowls.

When the week, that the vicar was due to attend the annual church conference, loomed ominously he enlisted Wilf's help.

Mrs Law and her two teenage sons were petrified with the thought of sharing their home with a devil for a week. Wilf assured the family that he would keep Angel locked in a shed and only feed and exercise him before dawn and after dark. Having faith in her husband's amazing control of cantankerous animals Mrs Law reluctantly agreed to the arrangement, but only for this emergency and for not one minute longer than a week.

Angel was duly collected on the morning of the vicar's departure. For the remainder of the day, he yelped, barked, snarled, growled and threw himself about in such a frenzy attempting to escape that many passers-by hurried along on the opposite side of the road.

At 5.30 the next morning a jagged hole at the foot of the shed door told Wilf that Angel was no longer a prisoner; and unless he was recaptured one whiff of such news around the village would bring it to a neurotic standstill.

Calculating that the dog would make tracks back to the vicarage, Wilf set off in search. The village was deathly quiet; even the dawn chorus seemed to be waiting expectantly. The regular squeak of a neglected bicycle wheel drew Wilf's attention towards Nathan, pushing his loaded carrier towards home after a successful nocturnal excursion.

"Seen anything of the vicars damn dog", he asked. "That I have, he's up around Top Meadow", replied Nathan. "Lucky he didn't see me".

A brisk ten minutes walk brought Wilf to Top Meadow and sure enough there was Angel half buried down a rabbit hole, a spray of soil jetting out behind him as if his front paws were mechanical diggers.

A curt command from Wilf brought Angel into reverse and obviously intent on extending his period of freedom.

Unfortunately for him his eyes met with the masters. He whimpered, shuddered from nose to tail then dropped prostrate onto his belly before crawling towards Wilf's feet.

Half an hour later the hole had been boarded over, and the escapee was safely back in his cell.

For the next few days all went well, even Mrs Law pushed food through to Angel on one occasion when Wilf was helping out at Bracken Ridge. In the middle of Thursday night, the Law family and all people living within half a mile distance were awakened by a maniacal outburst of barking from Angel with a rousing accompaniment from neighbouring hounds.

Wilf stumbled out into the yard and sensing that something was amiss released the dog. A couple of bounds took Angel to the gate and one huge leap took him over it into the road before he disappeared at high speed in the direction of Lower Wood.

The remainder of the night passed peacefully. At 7 a.m. Mrs Law looked out of the bedroom window then yelled downstairs to Wilf; "Half of the washings gone from the line, if it wasn't for that dog I'd have done it on Monday". "I'll let Constable Gwilt know", Wilf shouted back.

By mid-morning the village Constable had visited Mrs Law, written a few notes in his book and promised to do his best to recover the stolen clothes. The theft of a villagers washing became red alert and went straight to the top of his serious crime list.

The irritants that occasionally upset P.C. Gwilt's tranquil life in Tuttleborough were likely to be a drunk outside The Red Fox in need of an escort home, scrumping school boys needing their backsides kicking or generally keeping the peace when maundering farm animals blundered through cottage gardens. He had long ago given up doing battle with poachers. Some said he ate and slept better for it.

Wilf and his wife were at home, about to have afternoon tea, when P.C. Gwilt returned. The missing washing was tied neatly with a length of binder twine to the carrier at the back of his bike.

"That's a good day's work, where did you find them?" asked Mrs Law with obvious relief. "I noticed the gypsies had broken camp from down Lower Wood, so I followed them", explained the Constable. "Caught up with them the other side Clugton, by the way is that devil dog Angel back home yet?" "No! Can't find him anywhere", Wilf replied, "Why?" "Well the second van I looked in had the washing hidden away, but lying on his stomach on the bunk was a youth with a hole in his backside as big as a cricket ball". "Instant justice" Mrs Law muttered. "Quite often the best kind", agreed the Constable. Angel did return just before night fall, carrying a piece of well chewed coarse trouser fabric in his mouth and a strange look of satisfaction in his eyes.

As agreed, Wilf and Angel arrived at the vicarage at 9.o'clock the following Monday morning. Despite vigorous banging on the heavy oak door and a walk around the great stone house, there was no sign of the Reverend Sequera or his wife. The same procedure with the same results was followed that evening, and again the next morning.

Mrs Law issued her ultimatum after the third visit. "Get rid of that dog Wilf Law or I go and stay with mother until you do". There was a cold edge to her voice and Wilf knew that she meant it. Any regular routine kept by a villager was known to the minute by everyone else.

When the vicar arrived outside the church at precisely 10 o'clock on Wednesday morning he came face to face with Wilf and Angel sitting on the top step. His flowing cassock sagged to a wilt "Thought I might find you here vicar", Wilf greeted him dryly. "Ah! Wilf, I've been meaning to come and see you but I've been so busy", he flustered, his words spilling out like

100

released racing pigeons. "Hello Angel", he stretched out his hand to stroke the dog's head, but withdrew it smartly as a warning growl rumbled from somewhere behind the yellow fangs. "Well Wilf, I'd better confess it", he continued. "I failed, Angel and I will never see eye to eye and as for Mrs Sequera she's threatened to go to her mothers if I don't get rid of him. "That puts us both in the same boat vicar; my wife leaves tomorrow if I take him back home". "I think we need a miracle Wilf"

Wilf stood up and stretched to his full height of five feet nothing. "I think I might just have one up my sleeve vicar. Come on Angel". Looking puzzled but very relieved the reverend gentleman watched them walk through the grave yard and out under the lych gate.

As soon as his dad got back home young Tommy Law was sent of to find Jerry Bell, the gamekeeper.

Surrounded by seventy acres of woodland Jerry lived in a remote keeper's cottage a good cross-country distance out of the village. He had been head keeper for the Tuttleborough estate since the death of his father twenty six years past. Except for a black Labrador and a fox terrier, he lived on his own which probably accounted for the fact that he was a man who never used two words when one would suffice. The years he had spent so close to nature had taught Jerry to recognise and read the meaning of every animal track and call. He could mimic the song of every bird that visited the woods.

His living was spartan; he would eat no cooked food or brook any kind of artificial entertainment. Those who had good reason to know said that Jerry Bell could hear the crack of a twig above a howling gale at four furlongs distance.

Tommy found Jerry rewiring a pheasant pen, "Dad said would you call in to see him, it's urgent." "12 o'clock" Jerry continued working. Being a man where everything had to be uncomplicated and direct Jerry steadfastly followed the same code on his 1927 Triumph motorcycle, much to the annoyance of local landowners. He simply imagined a straight line from where he was to where he wanted to be and travelled it irrespective of the terrain.

At exactly twelve noon a motorcycle and its rider arrived in Wilf's back yard. "Well" was all Jerry said. "I heard that one of your dogs died last week Jerry" "Yup" "It's your lucky day; I've got a real good one to replace it" "Never" Jerry kick started his bike and would have been burning the grass across back field within seconds if Wilf had not stepped smartly in front of him. "You'll thank me for this before long Jerry Bell", he shouted as he picked up a rope that disappeared at its far end under the shed door and deftly tied it to the back of the motorbike. "Now get going" Wilf yelled as he lifted the latch.

Angel bounded out of the shed. Jerry took one look. The two words chosen to sum up his situation were drowned but the roar of the machine.

It was over a week later before Wilf and Jerry met up again.

"Sorry about that trick I played on you Jerry", he offered tentatively. Jerry stood silent for a long time, and then smiling broadly he proceeded to break his marathon speaking record. "Thanks Wilf, no more poachers" The news of Angel's change of address had spread rapidly round the village. Everyone had kept well away from the woods, and the vicar's orchard was added to the boys list of happy scrumping grounds.

GEORGE

Ralph Whittle could never say no. On many an occasion he had to collect his buck rake or seed drill from a neighbour's farm when he needed to use them himself. He had been known to loan Barney his champion Herefordshire bull to upgrade some of the inferior herds in the parish.

When the football team were looking for a new pitch it was Ralph who offered a field which was the nearest, but not that near to being the flattest piece of land locally.

It was no surprise to anyone when the Whittles agreed to take in one of the town lads for six months to gain agricultural experience before going on to college.

The callow sixteen year old youth, the son of a friend of Ralph's bank manager arrived at Hill Top with his suitcase late one Sunday evening as Ralph and Peggy returned home from chapel. Peggy had not met her new farmhand lodger previously and was surprised to see the ample frame he carried. At breakfast time next morning her surprise was even greater when she had to cook twice as much food as she normally did, to satisfy the needs of such a large body. By the end of the first week George had proved to be a quick learner and a very willing worker, much to Ralph's satisfaction.

Peggy, however, had in great dismay watched her larder stock dwindle alarmingly. The physical exertion in fresh country air had transformed George's initial lusty love of food into a voracious appetite which was proving difficult to accommodate. Peggy called her husband into private conference. "This can't go on much longer Ralph, he's eating us out of house and home, he should be named gorge, not George." "Leave it to me love, I'll think of something," Ralph promised.

That evening while checking the stock, Ralph decided to give George his first lesson in farm management. "Farming's a hard life, George," he began, "and to do well at it there are three important things to remember. Treat your livestock well, work with nature and make the best use of every minute of God's good time. It's the last point I want to discuss with you. Now that you're here to help for a few months, it seems to me that it's a waste of time you and me both breaking off for meals together, when one could be working while the other's eating." "Makes sense to me," agreed George. "So from tomorrow we can start a new efficiency drive. You come in first for breakfast; I come in first for tea. The missus will put your food on the corner table, anything on there is yours."

Peggy was happy with Ralph's diplomatic subterfuge. "I won't starve him," she promised, "just ration him a bit, I think he's been putting on weight." The plan worked to perfection. George did not complain about his restricted diet, and stability was returned to Peggy's larder.

The churchwomen's guild met on the second Thursday of every month in the front parlour at Hill Top. Once a hymn had been sung, prayers said and the business of cleaning rotas agreed, the afternoon was spent as a social gathering.

Mrs Whittle spent most of the morning preparing refreshments for the ladies. She liked to put on a good spread, introducing at least one new delicacy each month. The Midge sisters never missed a meeting only because of Peggy's culinary skills. They usually managed to eat twice as much as anyone else, but never offered one word of appreciation. After two hours of diligent preparation, plates of sausage rolls, ham sandwiches, scones, treacle cake and an assortment of fancy cakes surrounded a huge bowl of cream-topped fruit trifle on the corner table. All ready to be carried into the parlour that afternoon.

Peggy knew that the men were hay turning and would not be back before milking time. What she did not know was that Ralph had permitted George to knock off early so that he could go to town to buy his mother a birthday present. As the ladies settled for the meeting, George was one field away heading rapidly towards the farmhouse to change into his best clothes. He could hardly believe his eyes as he walked into the kitchen. Mrs Whittle has prepared me an early tea, he thought.

One hour later George was happily on his way to town and a bewildered Mrs Whittle was looking in disbelief at the sorry remains of the ladies' refreshments. One ham sandwich, two sausage rolls and a smattering of trifle around the edge of the bowl was all that remained.

Peggy's tearful indignation had not subsided as she recounted the incident to Ralph. Being a man with a rare talent for seeing the funny side of catastrophe, even when he hit his thumb with a hammer on a frosty morning, he burst out laughing.

"It's the last straw; he will have to go, tonight, as soon as he gets back. If you don't tell him then I will." Peggy delivered her edict with ice-cold determination.

As evening lengthened, dark clouds rolled over the hot, sticky day; sharp shafts of lightning following rumbling peels of thunder. As Ralph rose from his chair to look out towards the hayfield, the first raindrops splashed heavily against the window. "This should shrink young George before he gets back," Ralph joked. Peggy made no comment.

Just as the storm's momentum burst into its full sadistic mockery of haymaking time, the kitchen door crashed open and George stood one pace inside in a highly agitated state, little rivulets of water running from his hair down his suit onto the floor. "Mr Whittle," he gasped, "come quick, Captain's real sick." Ralph grabbed his coat from the back of the door and plunged his feet into his work boots. Ralph had great affection for all the farm livestock but his favourite by far was Captain, the gentle giant Clydesdale he had kept as a living link with the past. Now twenty four years old, he enjoyed his years of retirement out at pasture. "I've put him in the stable," George shouted against the storm as they splashed their way across the yard.

Captain was a forlorn sight in the light of the lantern. His head hung low, his breath came in erratic gasps and his body convulsed in violent shivers. "He won't last the night if we don't get the vet," said Mr Whittle, shaking his head ruefully. "I know where he lives, I'll get him," replied George. And he was running out of the stable back into the teeth of the storm before he could be stopped.

Captain had been rubbed down and covered with a thick blanket before the red Morris 7 pulled into the yard. Jim Foy the vet gave Captain a thorough examination, plunged a huge hypodermic needle into his withers, and then closed his bag.

"Can't be sure yet Ralph, could be colic. I'll call in again tomorrow morning." They walked together across to the car. "Good lad you got there, Ralph," Jim said, as he got behind the wheel. "Ask him what happened on his way over to my place."

Ralph plodded back to find George whispering words of encouragement and stroking the horse's neck. The lad stood in a pool of water, his new suit was absolutely sodden. "What happened to you then, young George?" "I took the short cut over Long Meadow then down the bank to Sandy Lane, but the footbridge collapsed and I fell in the brook," he replied sheepishly. "Good job it was raining then," Ralph quietly replied.

The Whittles agreed not to mention George's eating habits again. They tightened their belts and waited for September.

DEWDROP JENKS

Snowdrop and Dewdrop made the morning milk deliveries in Tuttleborough. Snowdrop, a gentle grey pony, pulled the float. Dewdrop Jenks slopped the milk into jugs and enamel tins, always remembering to add the extra drop.

Winter and summer alike, a glistening liquid pear-shaped diamond hung from the tip of his large, red nose, hence his nickname. For sixteen years the duo had done their daily round with hardly a variation. Without a word of command, snowdrop moved to and from the next customer with consummate patience, never putting a hoof wrong, until one morning in January 1936.

There had been eight days and nights of unrelenting, toe-tingling frost. The lanes were pock-marked with frozen potholes, the road a sheet of treacherous, silver-coloured ice. For two mornings Snowdrop had negotiated The Red Fox hill without mishap by descending it in a serpentine pattern. On the third morning her luck ran out. Halfway down, all four legs lost cohesion, sending her sprawling into the road.

"We had passed the pub, she was stone cold sober," Dewie joked weeks later. He heard the snap and knew immediately that his faithful little pony had broken a fetlock. With the help of Neb, Nathan and PC Gwilt, Snowdrop was released from the float and gently coaxed three-legged up to Pool Farm. "I can't afford the vet and I don't want her put down," Dewie told Ralph emphatically.

After a brief discussion it was decided to suspend the pony from the beams in the barn. A sling was made from an old Rick Sheet passed under Snowdrop's belly and the four men hauled on ropes until she dangled a few inches above the floor. A truss of hay and a water butt were placed within easy reach. With a length of drive belt canvas Ralph bound a pair of crude splints to the broken leg.

Dewie's problems were not over. He had to get a replacement for Snowdrop.
"I think I might be able to help there," offered Constable Gwilt, "meet me back at the float in an hour."

It was nearer two hours that Dewie saw the policeman coming up the hill pushing his bike with one hand while leading a mournful looking skewbald pony with the other.
"That's one of them gypsy ponies, isn't it?" mused Dewie in a voice edged with doubt. "Yep, Dewie, that it is, they owe me a few favours that lot do," was all the constable replied. With the

additional regular commands of "Wo-ah" and "Walk on", Dewie's routine with his new partner Skewie returned to normal.

Exactly one week from the day and at approximately the same time as Snowdrop had suffered her unfortunate accident, Jerry Bell the gamekeeper was cutting across ten acre field, a wash of ice crystals spraying from his back wheel, making a bee-line for home. The tall thorn hedge obscured the milk float from his sight until too late they met broadside at the open gate.

Jerry was launched as if by canon head first into the ditch, his bike landing on top of him. Skewie reared up wide-eyed, nostrils flared, churns clanked then fell, as Dewie valiantly held on to the bridle. Skewie's front legs clawed at the air then fell with a thud, landing directly on Dewie's leg.

Suffering only a few minor abrasions, Jerry hauled himself out of the ditch to calm the frightened animal. Dewie lay prostrate on the road.
"I think I've done a Snowdrop," he gasped, "I've broke me leg."

There was always help available for an emergency in Tuttleborough. Dewie was carefully lifted on to the back of the float to take him to the cottage hospital. Jerry volunteered to go ahead. He kicked up his motorbike; there was a belch of black smoke and a loud bang. Skewie already in a highly nervous state shied perpendicularly. Neb Straw reached for her head just as Dewie was catapulted off the back of the float. The pony backed up and a wheel ran over his good leg. "I think I've got a double Snowdrop," was all he said.

Billy Bufton took over the milk round while Dewie was recovering. Billy's smile just broadened when customers hinted at short measure, or the milk on the turn before it was delivered.

By late Spring, Dewie and Snowdrop were re-united. They both walked with a slight limp and took just a little longer to complete the daily milk round.

TUTTLEBOROUGH FC

The few matches played by the village football team each season were billed as friendlies. Demands made by seasonal work on the farms, sporadic hangovers, the pitch flooding in winter and a dearth of men at the age it is sensible to play such a dangerous game as village football, frequently made it difficult to field a full team.

By the end of October 1934, two matches had already been played. Both had been lost but the results were immaterial. The outcome of the next match against the old enemy Clugton was the only important one of the season.

It was quite normal for Tuttleborough to be fielding a team of seven or eight men as the referee's whistle blew. Before half-time latecomers had rushed in from the farms, shedding caps and jackets as they arrived ready to join the affray, with braces dangling. No-one ever wanted to play on the wing going downhill on the brook side flank as the ground was permanently boggy. Playing uphill on the opposite side only a player with one leg shorter than the other would have found it easy to keep balanced.

A week before the needle match was due to take place, Neb Straw at the Red Fox got a message from the opposition requesting a neutral referee. Neb enlisted the services of a publican acquaintance from town, on the promise of free ale after the game.

Clugton had won the last three fixtures against their local rivals, amassing sixteen goals against one in the process. Even that goal they bitterly disclaimed saying it had been kicked in by a spectator.

As match day drew near, Tuttleborough's determination to avenge the recent humbling defeats grew stronger. For the first time in the club's history a meeting was called to discuss tactics. Every play had his say, but finally it was agreed by everyone to adopt the style of play recommended by Harry Prince: "If you can't get the ball, get the man." After all, Harry had once been given a trial by Lovells Athletic.

Despite their dismal record of failure the villagers loyally supported the team and none so passionately as Mrs Aggy Spragg. Aggy, the wife of an abattoir slaughter man, had a limited vocabulary and an unlimited family of twelve. Her contribution to match proceedings was measured in quantity not quality.

The heavy rain that fell during the night preceding the match was welcomed by the team. Their lack of skill could now be blamed on the condition of the pitch. By three o'clock rival supporters were gathered along the touchline. Usually they segregated themselves by standing on opposite sides of the field from where they could safely throw insults; but the downpour had swollen the brook to within a foot of the playing area on this occasion.

Aggy by her very presence, a few mild insults and an entourage of followers had commandeered a prime spectators position on the halfway line. There were no spare balls for the teams to kick about before the game. The Clugton players stood in a huddle on the penalty spot listening to a last minute pep talk from the captain. The home side wandered around aimlessly dimping their last fags and occasionally kicking out at a cowpat. Mat Elms, supported by Aggy, stood on one leg, binding yards of binder twine around a boot with a dodgy sole. The twine procured from the bottomless pockets of Nathan's jacket.

Mark Sequera, the Vicar's son and team captain, won the toss at the third attempt. The first two spins of the coin landed edgeways on in the mud, known locally as a "butchers". He elected to play uphill first half.

For ten minutes the game was contested at fever pitch, both ball and players getting heavier with layers of mud every time they hit the pitch. The referee seemed disinclined to blow his whistle, correctly calculating that the poor physical condition of the ground and players could not withstand the tempo for long.

A brief reprise came when Roy Ankers wellied the ball into the brook, then refused to uphold the time-honoured rule of "he who wellies it in, gets it out". He was soon persuaded to follow tradition by Mrs Spragg, fearing her wrath much more than the cold water.

Miraculously no-one sustained serious injury from the tackles that went in with arms and legs flailing like a harvest binder. With half-time imminent to the point where the referee had raised his whistle, Ron Nogrove smashed a shot with ferocious power striking the unfortunate man on the back of his head. For a split second be became airborne, arms and legs splayed out like a hovering bird of prey. Seconds later he was lying face down prostrate in a sea of oozing mud. Hip flasks appeared as if by magic, one was seen to be pulled from the goalkeeper's back pocket. Recovered but unwilling to return to the field of battle, the referee handed in his whistle.

Ron and his lethal left foot had a reputation. He carried too much excess weight to actually take part in the game, but when the ball came near him it was prudent for all players to get out of the way. In the past he had broken two crossbars, the fingers of three goalkeepers and left permanent lace imprints on the backside of an opposing centre forward. He had however scored three goals last season, one of which was for his own team.

The match was about to be abandoned when the Rev. Sequera volunteered to take the whistle. Being a man of the cloth the visitors agreed. The vicar controlled the second half very well except that following every infringement he issued a mini sermon to the perpetrator.

Having the advantage of playing downhill Tuttleborough enjoyed almost all of the attacking play, but never having managed to master the slope, all efforts at goal went flying wide and high. The game was petering out to an honourable draw when on a rare visit into the penalty area the Clugton inside right was unceremoniously scythed down by a Billy Bufton special. Billy's face glowed with the broad smile of one who had just achieved a great victory. The blast of the whistle and the vicar's finger pointing to the penalty spot caused pandemonium amongst the spectators. Shouts of "I should think so, Ref", "about time too" and "well done, Vicar" peeled out from the visiting supporters. All but one from Tuttleborough stood in abject disbelief. The poor vicar's eyesight, intelligence, age, even religion, was brought into question by the outraged Aggy Spragg.

Ted Yapp the goalkeeper had become an instant hero in the last game of the previous season when he saved a critical penalty shot in the last minute of the game. He did not intend to, and probably would not have done, if he had not when assuming a menacing, panther-like crouch, broken wind aggressively. The opposing player had been so surprised by such an unexpected occurrence that he completely lost control of himself shooting tamely into Ted's hands.

He decided to attempt a repeat performance. Ted assumed the same intimidating stance but try as he might; the deathly silence was broken only by a toot on the ref's whistle and the whoosh of the ball as it flashed past him. Chugton supporters were jubilant.

Tuttleboroughs despondent: except for one. Aggy was advancing rapidly on the Rev. Sequera. One look at her face distorted with anger was enough. Lacking the protection of his pulpit, the vicar made a hasty retreat towards the footbridge. Adrenalin running at the speed of floodwater gave Aggy amazing acceleration. She caught the reverend gentleman as he stepped on to the rickety plank and with one mighty swipe of her right arm intended to send him plunging into the brackish depths. Fortunately for the vicar he ducked and the impetus of her haymaking right swing sent Aggy spinning from the bridge into the brook. Spluttering with indignation Aggy surfaced only to see the vicar's wagging finger, "Love thine enemies, Mrs Spragg, love thine enemies," he shouted.

Mark had rapidly arrived on the scene to give support to his father, but seeing no ill-effects, offered the olive branch to Aggy by holding out a helping hand. She grabbed the hand and with a sudden tug brought Mark somersault fashion to join her in the water.

Gleefully she looked towards the Rev. Sequera, "And the sins of the father will be visited upon the son," she shouted triumphantly.

Printed in the United Kingdom
by Lightning Source UK Ltd.
117516UKS00001B/115-150